P9-DBY-276

ONE BOY, NO WATER

This book is a work of fiction. Names, characters, places, and incidents either are products of the author's imagination or are used fictitiously. Any resemblance to actual events or locales or persons, living or dead, is entirely coincidental and not intended by the author.

Copyright © 2012 by Lehua Parker, LLC
Illustration © 2012 by Corey Egbert

All rights reserved. Except as permitted under the U.S. Copyright Act of 1976, no part of this publication may be reproduced, distributed, or transmitted in any form or by any means, or stored in a database or retrieval system, without the prior return permission of the publisher. The scanning, uploading, and distribution of this book via the Internet or via any other means without the permission of the publisher is illegal and punishable by law. Please purchase only authorized electronic editions and do not participate in or encourage electronic piracy or copyrighted materials. Your support of the author's rights is appreciated.

Second paperback edition: January 2014

Hawaiian proverbs used with permission by:
Pukui, Mary Kawena. 'Ōlelo Noeau: Hawaiian Proverbs & Poetical Sayings. Honolulu: Bishop Museum Press, 1983.

For information on subsidiary rights, please contact the publisher at rights@jollyfishpress.com. For a complete list of our wholesalers and distributors, please visit our website at www.jollyfishpress.com.
For information, address Jolly Fish Press, PO Box 1773, Provo, UT 84603-1773.

Printed in the United States of America

Paperback ISBN: 978-1-939967-78-7

THIS TITLE IS ALSO AVAILABLE AS AN EBOOK.

10 9 8 7 6 5 4 3 2 1

For my mother, Katherine Frampton Covalt, who bought me a typewriter one Christmas with the vision she'd one day read a book, and for my father, Stephen H. Covalt, who now calls me Da Shark Lady.

PRAISES FOR *ONE BOY, NO WATER*

"... *One Boy, No Water* is a colorful island tale and a modern take on various aspects of Hawaiian legend. . . . Lehua Parker has written a lovely book for an age group often ignored."
—*Hawaii Reads*

"... original, magic, true, funny, and hard to put down."
— Sue Cowing, award-winning author of *You Will Call Me Drog* and *My Dog has Flies: Poetry For Hawaii's Kids*

"What made this story special for me was the window it provided into the society of island children as they struggle for self-identity in the often confusing chop suey mix of multi-ethnicity and pecking order politics."
— Kirby Wright, author of *Punahou Blues* and *Moloka'i Niu Ahina*

"Parker does an amazing job of weaving the mystery of who and what Zader is throughout the story. Even more outstanding is her ability to infuse other mythologies into the action, which only serve to heighten the secrecy surrounding Zader. The truth will boggle the mind."
—Ann-Marie Meyers, author of *Up in the Air*

"Lehua Parker hits one out of the park with *One Boy, No Water* ... She absorbs the reader in the story to the extent they forget it is a children's book. [Her] debut novel dangles the bait, sets the hook, reels us in."
—Penny Freeman, editor-in-chief, *Xychler Publishing.*

NIUHI SHARK SAGA

BOOK ONE

ONE BOY, NO WATER

A NOVEL
BY
LEHUA PARKER

Illustrated by
Corey Egbert

JOLLY
FISH
PRESS
Provo, Utah

A Note from Aunty Lehua

Aloha!

The *Niuhi Shark Saga* takes place in an imaginary town on Oahu, Hawaii, called Lauele. Like most islanders, the characters sometimes use common Hawaiian and Hawaiian Pidgin English words and phrases. Most of the time it's easy to figure out the meaning from the context. For example, *plenny small kine fish* translates into *plenty of small kinds of fish*.

However, some words like *hanai* (adopted) or *ohana* (family) are harder to figure out. But don't worry, there's a glossary at the end of the book that explains the non-standard English words. If you have a question, be sure to check there. There's also a Pidgin dictionary, free reader's guide, and more activities on www.NiuhiSharkSaga.com.

I hope *One Boy, No Water* gives you a little taste of island living. Drop me a line and tell me what you thought. I love to hear from readers.

A hui hou,

Aunty Lehua
AuntyLehua@NiuhiSharkSaga.com
www.NiuhiSharkSaga.com
www.LehuaParker.com

1
THE END OF SUMMER FUN

~Like beef?: an invitation to a fight, not dinner.~

"**Z**ader, like play?" my almost twin brother Jay asked. I was sitting under the monkey pod tree by the soccer field, drawing lines with an old popsicle stick. It was the last day of our last year of Summer Fun and I wanted to go home already. "Zader?" Jay said.

"What?" I didn't look up.

"Do you wanna play? Frankie and me and you against Jerry, Carson, and Benji. Shambattle. Down by the tetherball pole. No sprinklers over there." Juggling a red playground ball, Jay jerked his head toward the courts.

I flicked my eyes to the sky, considering. I wasn't wearing my rain jacket, and playing shambattle meant my umbrella would be on the ground out of reach, but with clear skies and no chance of sprinklers suddenly turning on, I should be okay. I shrugged my shoulders and dropped the stick.

Beats scratching like a chicken in the dirt, I thought.

"Nah, Jay," drawled Chad Watanabe from the picnic table, "You're wasting your time asking Zader. Zader can't handle shambattle with the boys. He's a runner, not a fighter. Chasemaster with the girls is more his style."

Great, I thought, one-note-Chad getting ready to sing his favorite tune: "Mess with Zader" by the Mouth Breathers.

Jay didn't even turn around. "Shut your face, Chad."

"What you said, stupid-head?" Tunazilla lurched up from the under the slide where she'd been counting ukus.

It's alive.

"N-n-nothing," Chad said, backpedaling.

Making fun of me was one thing; getting on Tunazilla's girl-power radar just cranked Chad's little man taunting game into the big leagues.

"Chad said girls are lame," Jay smirked. "They can't play shambattle like boys. Sic 'em, Tuna."

Like a giant gecko under a heat lamp, Tunazilla blinked and turned her big head toward Chad, cupping her right hand into a loose fist as she spoke. "So girls are only good at running away, hah? You wanna see what a girl can handle? You like beef?"

"N-n-no," said Chad. "I wasn't talking about you, Tunazil—uh, I mean, Petunia."

She nodded. "So you no like beef?"

Chad looked at her hands, the size of baseball mitts, and blanched. "No way! I was talking about Zader. He's the runner."

"Yeah, he's not a tough tita like you, Tunazilla!" laughed Alika Kanahele, Chad's BFF. Like hyenas, they hunted as a pack. Chad was slighter and sneakier and smart enough to leave most of the heavy lifting to Alika. Alika was Petunia's cousin and the only person in the world who would dare call her Tunazilla to her face. Held back in third grade, he towered over everybody except Tuna and liked to stand too close.

Still grinning, Alika turned toward me and away from the picnic table where he'd been using his broken utility knife to carve something witty like his initials. All summer long he'd hid the blade from Mr. Tony, our twenty-something Summer Fun Leader. Whenever Mr. Tony and Jay were busy, Alika liked to wave his knife at me and pretend to slit his throat.

Well, *my* throat, technically.

Ignore it. I thought, as Alika flashed his knife at me for the third time that week. Thoughts chased like schools of fish through my head. *Tell Jay. Tell Mr. Tony. Maybe one of these times he'll actually do it.*

I glanced back to our classroom where Mr. Tony was counting the juice money with bossy Lisa Ling and my calabash cousin Char Siu Apo. Since the beginning of Summer Fun Lisa had campaigned hard for the title of teacher's pet, always wiping the whiteboards with their special cleaner, making sure everybody stayed in line on the way to the cafeteria, and deciding who got a bathroom pass. I don't know why Char Siu tagged along; she didn't need to stand in Lisa's shadow. With the three of them working on it, it wouldn't take long to get the juice order ready to turn into the office. I figured Alika and Chad had maybe five more minutes before Mr. Tony and the girls came walking out. I turned my attention back to Alika.

Not enough time to make serious trouble, but I'm keeping an eye on him.

"What're you looking at?" Alika sneered.

Stay chilly, I thought. *It's all words.*

Walking towards me, but hiding the knife from Jay, Alika called, "Eh, Tuna! Chad's wrong to call Zader a girl. He's not like girls either. The reason Zader can't handle shambattle with the boys is because he's a panty. Girls *get* panty. That's the difference."

"Good one, Alika!" Chad snorted. "Whop yo' jaws, Zader!"

So funny I forgot to laugh, I thought. I gritted my teeth, picked up the stick, and started poking at the dirt again. *Just five more minutes. I can do anything for five minutes.*

But my hanai brother Jay would never take crap for a second, let alone five minutes.

"Shut up, Alika," Jay snapped. "No one was talking to you."

"No one was talking to Darth Zader either," Alika retorted. "Loser."

Chad laughed and started sucking air in and out like a scuba diver, his best attempt at a Darth Vader impersonation.

Like I haven't heard that one before.

"Wow, when you make that sound it's so natural, Chad," Jay said. "Sounds like you're stupid fo'real."

Chad stood up. "What did you say?"

"Ha! Deaf, too?"

"Jay," called Frankie, bouncing another ball. "We playing or what?"

"Yeah," Jay answered, never taking his eyes off Chad or Alika. "We're gonna play. You coming, Z?"

I checked the clouds again, white and fluffy and clinging to the pali cliffs far away. I nodded and picked up my umbrella.

Anything to get out of here.

I was walking toward Jay when it happened.

Alika threw a Dixie cup of water on me.

"Zader!" Jay shrieked.

The water hit my left shoulder. Hot lava fingers oozed down, scalding, sizzling, burning everything in its path like acid. Like snake venom. Like death. On fire, I dropped to the ground and rolled.

"Awesome, Alika!" Chad crowed. "Check it! It's just like holy water on a devil!"

Wide-eyed, Alika crossed himself. "He's possessed!" he shouted. "Everybody, Zader's possessed!"

Through the pain, I felt Jay kneel next to me, his hands ripping at the bottom of my t-shirt. "Zader, off! Get it off! Lift your arms so I can get it off." As he threw the shirt over my head, I felt a final sting as a wet sleeve brushed against my face, raising another angry line of welts along my cheekbone. More shadows ringed me.

Please don't let me barf, I prayed.

I swallowed hard as Jerry Santos and Benji Chang looked down, mouths open and catching flies. When I was sure breakfast was staying put, I pushed Jay away and stood up, covering the weeping sores and broken blisters with my hands.

Exposed!

Alika jammed his knife back into his pocket, jumped up on the picnic table bench, and thrust out his arms, making the sign of the cross with his index fingers. "You stay away from me, Zader, you freak," he yelled.

Jay didn't yell back, but launched himself at Alika, knocking the fat bully off the bench. He sat on Alika's stomach, cranked his fist back, and POW! He broke Alika's nose.

"Owweeeeeee!" Alika squealed.

"Confunit!" Mr. Tony charged out of the classroom door late as always, the girls flowing behind and around him like bees from a hive.

"Jay punched Alika!" Chad tattled, already scrambling to cover his 'okole.

Mr. Tony reached down and pulled Jay away. He grabbed my wet shirt, snapped it once to get the dirt off, and used it to mop up the blood from Alika's gushing nose.

I'm never wearing that again.

Jay stood breathing like bull and clenching his fist.

"You're not supposed to say confunit," Lisa Ling said, tucking the juice money box under her arm. "It's Pidgin. We're supposed to speak English at school."

"Oh, give it a rest, Lisa," Char Siu said. "We may be at Lauele Elementary, but it's Summer Fun, not school!"

"Sorry," Mr. Tony said. "But confunit, what's going on?"

On the ground Alika wailed like a tsunami siren.

"Jay punched Alika!" Chad shouted again.

"I can see that, Captain Obvious. Why?" Mr. Tony asked.

"Because he's mental," Chad said, "just like his freaky brother. Alika never did anything."

"Alika threw water on Zader," Frankie chimed in.

"Zader's got blisters," Benji said. "Look."

"Blisters? From what?"

Jay hissed, "Zader's allergic to water! Everybody knows he gets blisters when he gets wet. He can't get wet. It would kill him." Jay, my champion as surely as if he'd been riding a white horse, was deeply, thoroughly ticked. He ran his bloody knuckles through his hair, trying to keep it together, but I could tell he was about to snap. Words were nothing compared to water, and Alika'd crossed the line.

"What? I never knew Zader was allergic to water!" Mr. Tony said. "Oh, enough already, Alika." He sat him up.

Alika hiccupped and gasped for air.

Who's the panty now?

Mr. Tony pulled my bloody t-shirt away from Alika's nose. "Huh. Maybe you better go to the office." He leaned closer. "I think it's broken."

"Owweeeeeee!" Alika ramped up again.

As bad as it was, Alika was lucky. If Jay hadn't needed to take care of me first, along with his broken nose, Alika would be spitting out teeth after choking down the Dixie cup. He'd be breathing through his ear. I smiled.

"Shhhhhh." Mr. Tony clamped my t-shirt back on Alika's face. "Quiet. You're going to make it bleed more. Chad, take Alika to the office."

"What's that thing on Zader's back?" Becky Waters asked. "It's gross!"

My birthmark! I'm not wearing a shirt!

"Shut up, Becky!" said Char Siu. "What's that on your face?"

"Freckles aren't like that! That thing looks like a giant triangle tattoo. No wonder Zader always wears a shirt."

"You're being rude!" Char Siu snapped. "It's a birthmark, not a tattoo!"

"Check out Zader's blisters," whispered Lisa.

I looked at my shoulder and through my fingers I could see the blisters shrinking, forming pox marks of gray, scaly skin. Like a sunburn on hyper drive, these patches hid smooth healthy skin underneath. I brushed my fingers and thin gray flakes fell like confetti.

"Ewww!" Lisa gagged. "That's skin!"

"No way I'm walking by the monkey pod tree ever again," Becky shuddered.

"Shut-up," said Char Siu. "Where's your manners?"

I turned away, hiding my birthmark where they couldn't see.

Just let me disappear.

But then Alika spotted my birthmark in all its blue-black glory. "Mmmnevvvillll!" he shouted through my blood-soaked t-shirt, his arm stretched out toward me, finger pointing like the judgment of God.

"What?" Lisa asked.

"He called my cousin a devil," explained Char Siu as she drew back her foot. "And that's really rude!"

"Charlene Suzette Apo!" cried Mr. Tony.

"Owweeeeeee!" Alika scrambled, trying to protect both his bleeding nose and bruising shin with his hands. Chad stepped close, hooked Alika's arm around his neck, and turned him toward the office.

"Ha-la, Alika!" Tunazilla rumbled from her lair beneath the slide. "You gonna get plenny lickings tonight! Just wait until Tutu sees your face!"

Mr. Tony said, "Zader, I need you to—"

If I'm a devil, I can just leave, I thought. What's Mr. Tony going to do? Throw more water on me? Make me stay another day in Summer Fun? I don't care if I'm busted. Jay can play shambattle with his friends. I'm outta here.

Still rubbing my shoulder, I turned away from their stares and ignored Mr. Tony's calls. I started towards home, the sun warm and bright on my bare back, my umbrella abandoned under the monkey pod tree.

2
TALKING STORY

"**E**h, Z-boy, howzit?" Uncle Kahana said. He and Ilima, his yellow poi dog, were coming back from the ocean, walking around the naupaka kahakai bushes that separated the beach from the road. Long before I saw them, I smelled the fresh fish in his net bag as it dripped saltwater and blood into the dust by the roadside. I shuddered and tried not to watch each drop as it grew fat and fell.

"Howzit, Uncle Kahana," I said, looking everywhere but the bag.

Uncle Kahana paused, giving me a sharp once over. "Why aren't you wearing a shirt? Where's your umbrella, hah?" he badgered. "Your mom's going to flip if she finds out you're running around without it. Wait. Summer Fun's not over yet. Where's Jay?"

I shrugged. It was easier than trying to explain.

He narrowed his eyes at me. "Don't give me that," he said. "What happened?"

"Jay punched Alika Kanahele and gave him a bloody

nose. Mr. Tony, the Summer Fun guy, took my shirt to stop the bleeding."

Uncle Kahana's eyes narrowed even more. Ilima chuffed. "I know, girl, he's not telling the whole story, and the parts that're missing are the most important parts."

He tilted his head to the side. "Tell me, Z-boy. I can't help if I don't know."

You also can't hurt if you stay out of it, I thought and sighed.

"My house," said Uncle Kahana. "We'll talk story there."

UNCLE KAHANA AND ILIMA LIVED in an apartment above Hari's, a store bigger than an ordinary neighborhood convenience store, but not as big as a supermarket. Hari's carried a little bit of everything, from octopus lures and crack seed to 'ukulele strings, motor oil, and macadamia nut candies for tourists. It didn't make sense that Uncle Kahana lived there and got everything at Hari's for free. When I asked, Mom said Hari and Uncle Kahana had been in the war together and to stop being so niele.

Grown-ups. Everything's a mystery.

We walked around the side of Hari's store to the back lanai, a covered porch area with a sink, hose bib, table, and folding chairs. He tossed me a clean shirt from the clothesline. "Put this on."

"Thanks." It was big, but much better than nothing. As much as I hated wearing jackets and carrying an umbrella, I hated people staring at my birthmark even more.

At least Uncle Kahana cares, I thought.

Uncle Kahana placed his net bag with the fish in the sink and motioned toup the stairs attached to the side of the building. "Go on up. It's not locked. Ilima and I gotta clean up a little first." He waited until I was halfway up the stairs before turning on the hose.

"Come on, Ilima, don't be a baby," Uncle Kahana said.

She whined.

"No, the water's not that cold. Look, I'll go first."

Ilima barked.

"What're you talking about? Of course you need to rinse off! I don't want hairy salt all over the place."

Bark, bark, bark!

"So stay outside in the sun for a while. Dry off."

Whine. Chuff.

"Codeesh, Ilima! Stop acting like a diva-lani! I'm not going to heat the water for you! Come on! Zader's waiting!"

I kicked off my slippahs and entered the apartment. The main area was a large room split into a living room and kitchen-dining space. Uncle Kahana's furniture was old, but comfortable.

To the left of the entry was the living room with its brown, fake leather couch piled high with throw pillows in bright Hawaiian prints and a sliding glass door that led to a narrow ocean-view lanai that formed the roof of the front overhang of the store. To the right was a dining table and chairs nestled in front of a bachelor's bare bones kitchen and breakfast counter. Along the back wall between the kitchen and living room was a short hallway that led to

Uncle Kahana's bedroom, bath, and a large storage closet. Directly in front of the entry and almost blocking the way was Ilima's pillow, the center and heart of the home.

"Fine," said Uncle Kahana as he climbed the steps. "You can stay outside on the landing and guard the slippahs. Nobody wants a wet dog in the house."

I stepped away from the entry to make room for Uncle Kahana. He walked through the door wiping his arms on an old hammajang towel. Flicking his slippahs off, he turned back towards the door.

Ilima slunk up the stairs, tail and ears dripping and drooping. She plopped down in the sun outside the front door, eyeing her pillow in the house longingly.

"I said when you're dry."

Ilima sighed a huge doggy sigh.

"Look, I'll leave the door open so you can still hear what's going on."

Ilima closed her eyes and sighed again.

"No act Ilima," said Uncle Kahana. "Like you never take a bath every time we come back from the beach!"

Uncle Kahana turned to me. "Sit, sit, sit." He flapped his hands at the couch. "You look like you could use a drink. I'll check the ice box."

I moved some pillows to make room, and Uncle Kahana rummaged through the fridge, pulling out two Diamond Head orange sodas. He popped the tops and took the time to wrap one in a paper towel and slipped it into a plastic shopping bag before handing it over. Unlike most people, Uncle Kahana thought about things like condensation dripping off a cold soda can. He grabbed a straw off the counter and stuck it in my drink.

"Mahalo, Uncle," I said. The soda was cold and sweet and 'ono in the back of my throat.

Uncle Kahana carried a dining room chair over to the couch and sat backwards, his arms resting on the chair back. He took a sip of soda, then eyed me over the can. "Spill it," he said.

Or what?

I fiddled with the plastic bag, adjusting it tighter around the can, wiggled my 'okole deeper into the couch, and plopped my bare feet on the coffee table. I looked out the lanai door and watched a couple of clouds head mauka where I hoped they would eventually drop their rain down the steep mountainsides and not on Lauele when it was time to walk home. My hand twitched at the thought, and I regretted leaving my umbrella under the monkey pod tree.

Through it all Uncle Kahana sat quietly in his chair, occasionally lifting his drink, looking like he had nothing better to do or no place he'd rather be. On the landing Ilima rolled on her back and snoozed in the sunshine, legs up like a dead cockaroach.

I took a deep breath, opened my mouth, and it all rushed out like the big, rolling breakers at Nalupuki beach. "Alika Kanahele and Chad Watanabe were hassling me. No big deal. I knew Mr. Tony—our Summer Fun Leader—would be out on the playground soon. I was just going to ignore them, but like always, Jay jumped to the rescue and told them to stop it. That's when Alika threw a cup of water on me."

Uncle Kahana's eyebrows raised and Ilima sat up, but nobody said anything. I held out my arm and turned my shoulder toward him, lifting up the t-shirt sleeve. He rubbed his hand on his pants to make sure it was dry before reaching out to slowly trace the faintly pink skin, all that was left of the blisters and pain. Satisfied, he nodded and gestured at me to continue.

"Jay ripped my shirt over my head and that stopped the burning. I couldn't think about anything but the pain. I never had that much water on my skin before." I swallowed, the words choking like sand in my throat. Alika was laughing, making the sign of the cross at me with his fingers like I was a vampire."

Warm and dry from the sun and smelling clean from her bath, Ilima padded in, jumped up next to me on the couch, and rested her head in my lap. I started to pet her ears, smoothing the hair down, down, down, allowing the words to come.

"Alika called me a freak. Said I was possessed. Jay just snapped. He jumped Alika, knocked him down, sat on his chest, and pounded his face. Blood everywhere. I think Jay broke Alika's nose. Mr. Tony ended the fight and used my shirt to stop the bleeding. He sent Alika and Chad to the office. Even though Jay threw the punch, everybody was staring at me and my blisters, so I left."

"Drink," Uncle Kahana said. "It'll help."

I chugged half the soda, feeling the chill fall all the way to the pit of my stomach. It rumbled a bit, wanting more than sugar and fizz.

"Alika and Chad, they do this a lot when Jay's not around." Not a question from Uncle Kahana, but a certainty.

I nodded.

"The water?"

"No. First time. People know about my allergies, but most have never seen what happens."

"Plenny people saw today."

"Yeah."

"And Jay? What about his part in all this?" Uncle Kahana leaned toward me across the back of his chair.

He was casual, too casual, and I knew there was something deeper here, hidden like wana in the reef. I mentally stepped back and thought about what actually happened. By sticking up for me, Jay had inadvertently escalated the conflict. Before he stuck his nose in my kimchee, it was only words, words I'd heard a million times before, and not just from Alika and Chad. The problem was that Jay never heard those kinds of words from anybody and didn't think I should either.

Everybody naturally *liked* Jay. He thought I needed him around for protection, but what I really needed was his ability to act as a buffer between me and the rest of the world. Around Jay I got invited to shambattle; without him all people saw was a freak.

I shrugged. "He's my brother," I said, and that said it all.

I felt Uncle Kahana relax. I wondered if I'd passed some kind of test, but for what, I couldn't imagine.

"Uncle Kahana? Are they right? Am I a freak?"

Uncle Kahana ran his hand over his face and studied the picture of Diamond Head on his can. Finally, he said, "I ever tell you about the day I found you at Piko Point?"

3
MANO MEAL

~Keiki ho'okama: a child one loves and considers family but usually does not raise; a godchild.~

Eleven years ago, Kahana Kaulupali walked toward the ocean, his slippahs flip, flip, flipping sand behind him. Ilima bounded ahead, nosing around gray driftwood and seaweed as she picked her way to the water.

"Ho, Ilima, careful where you put your nose, yeah? Better watch out for jellyfish! I bet those buggers washed up on the beach last night."

Ilima looked back and whined.

"Nah, Sister, don't worry. I have meat tenderizer." Kahana patted his bag. "Gets rid of the sting in nothing flat."

Ilima chuffed and went back to work.

Overhead, a seabird called as it headed out to sea. The sun was over the mountains, the pale shell colors of early dawn giving way to a brilliant blue sky as the sun began to shine in earnest. Carrying his fishing spear and the bag with his fins and mask in one hand and tossing his hammajang beach towel over his shoulder, Kahana settled his slippahs deeper into the night-cooled sand at Keikikai beach and surveyed his domain.

Up the beach, past the ancient lava flow that divided Keikikai and Nalupuki beaches, the waves were unseasonably small for Nalupuki, not worth the time for local surfers chasing bigger rides. At his feet, Keikikai was its usual kid-friendly calm with waves no bigger than ripples inside the reef. The water was crystal clear to its sand bottom, perfect for spearfishing lazy parrot fish or octopus nestled in crevasses along the reef's edge.

On this easy Sunday morning no joggers or beachcombers roamed the shore, and the sand was barren of footprints as far as his eyes could see. Except for a few tipped over beer bottles and a fast food wrapper, the parking lot at the beach pavilion was empty. It wouldn't take long for families with coolers and boogie boards to appear, but for now the entire shoreline belonged to Kahana and Ilima, just the way they liked it.

Another beautiful day in Hawaii nei, thought Kahana. *Time to spear a fish.*

Still, as eager as he was to dive into the ocean and stroke seal-sleek along the reef, Kahana paused. He slipped his towel off his shoulder and stood looking toward Piko Point, the farthest tip of the lava flow that jutted from the shoreline and into the deep. Something wasn't quite right.

Keeping his breathing slow and even, Kahana tried not to count each wave that sloshed at his toes or think about the way his pulse beat like a hula dancer's drum in his temple. He focused on the tide coming in and watched the small band of churning sand that separated the ocean from the shore. The breeze was gentle and soothing, and the ocean reflected the impossible blue of the sky.

It's perfect, he thought. *So why do I feel like a crab inching toward a fish gut-baited trap?*

Kahana shaded his eyes and scanned the horizon. Whatever it was, it was out in the water. Ilima wandered back from the ocean's edge and sat at Kahana's feet, ignoring the waves sweeping back and forth as she scratched behind her ear.

"What you think, eh, Ilima? Good day for spearing a fish?" Ilima whined and leaned against Kahana's leg. In the hot sun, Kahana shivered. "Yeah, I know, I know. You feel 'em too, Ilima. Something's out there, something that wants to eat a skinny old man. We better stay on the rocks today."

Kahana rubbed his chicken skin arms, but the goose bumps wouldn't settle. He hefted his fishing spear and adjusted his towel on his shoulder.

"Come, Ilima, let's go."

With a head jerk, Kahana and Ilima headed toward the lava rocks. The lava flow curved as it reached into the ocean, cupping Keikikai like a long fingered hand, shielding it from the wild open ocean currents that pounded Nalupuki's shore.

Striding across the first slippery finger, Kahana saw movement out the corner of his eye, a quick, angry flick of a tail near the far edge of the reef at Piko Point. Moving his hand to block the sun, he spotted a dark bullet shape cruising along the inside reef on the Keikikai side and heading toward the beach.

Kalei-O-Mano, he thought. *No wonder I have chicken skin!*

"I knew it, Ilima! Kalei-O-Mano was just hoping to catch me in the water!" Kahana narrowed his eyes as the Niuhi shark cruised along the reef, nosing into pockets and hollows as if searching for a snack. "See the top of his tail? See the piece missing? That's how I know it's Kalei."

He cocked his head to the side and bit the end of his thumb. "But why is he hanging around a kids' beach after all these years? Last I heard, Niuhi sharks hunt around one of the northern islands near Respite Beach. More remote out there, better game. I don't like that he's back in Lauele in the daylight, Ilima."

Ilima barked a quick jagged yelp and growled low in her throat.

Kahana's vision blurred as he remembered the way Keikikai beach looked the last time Kalei hunted here, the water red with lehua blossoms of blood that floated in with the tide to stain the sand.

"The last time Kalei was here he was all tangled up in a hukilau net. My father sliced his tail fin getting him out." Kahana shook his head. "I've never seen a shark that angry; I thought he was going ram our boat and sink it, but he didn't. We should've died that day, Ilima. You, me, and Daddy, too."

Kalei-O-Mano circled closer to the edge of the reef and rolled to his side, his eye looking back at Kahana on the rocks.

"Ho, Ilima, Kalei's humongous now! Bigger than Jaws, I think!"

Knowing better than to shout Kalei's true name, Kahana called out to sea, "Eh, Jaws Junior! Long time no see! Let's keep it that way, hah?"

At his shout, the enormous shark surfaced and flicked his tail in disdain, his sharp dorsal fin slicing through the calm waters. Raising his massive head out of the water, he barred his teeth, then sank back like a freight train disappearing down a tunnel.

Kahana waited, scanning the water and reef.

Sharks, he thought. *Like the ocean, it's never a good idea to stand with your back towards them.*

He watched the ocean for another moment or two until the feeling of dread eased, releasing its grip on his guts. His chicken skin relaxed, a sure sign that Kalei had moved out to deeper water.

Gone.

Kahana let the air out of his lungs with a whoosh and pretended his knees weren't wobbly. "Well, Ilima, it looks like Kalei no like beef today."

Ilima chuffed.

Peeling a strip of thumbnail with his teeth and putting it carefully into his pocket—kahunas and sorcerers were rare these days, but old habits die hard—he watched the clouds on the horizon, thinking. He reached down and idly patted Ilima's head.

"Niuhi! Here, on Keikikai? Odd, yeah, Ilima? All the big fish are on the deep water side of the reef past Nalupuki's second break. Nothing on this side of the reef would make a mouthful."

Ilima looked up, sneezed, then moseyed along the rocks, looking for something interesting to roll in.

"Nothing except people, I mean," Kahana said. "But there's no reason for that. Biting people causes more trouble than it's worth. Nobody knows that better than Kalei." Kahana shook his head.

Ilima chuffed and yawned.

"Chee, maybe we should just bag it and leave the reef for another day. I think there's some ripe papaya by Nakamura's side fence. Plus we have a ton of green mangoes from Liz. Taste real good with a little shoyu."

Absentmindedly, Kahana scratched his chest and watched the water flow over the reef and onto the sand. *Not a day for spearfishing*, he thought, *not a day for anything. Everything's a little bit off.*

Carried by the ocean breeze, the sound rose and fell so softly that at first Kahana thought he was imagining it. "What the—"

In a flash, Ilima took off for Piko Point, the last finger of lava that pointed the way out past the reef and into the deep, deep, deep.

"Ilima! Careful! If you slip you'll end up a Niuhi Scooby snack! Kalei's sly, you know. It might be a trick to get us into the water! Slow down!"

Kahana hustled after Ilima, his rubber slippahs wrapping around sharp points of lava, sliding over seaweed-slick patches, and splashing through shallow tide pools of warm, salty water. A hard knot formed in his stomach and pushed into his throat.

What cries like a newborn baby and lives on the reef?

In the distance Ilima wagged her tail as she licked something over and over, pausing only to bark at him to hurry, hurry, hurry up.

"So what, you think you're Lassie now?" puffed Kahana. Climbing over a jagged bulge of lava and skirting the last tide pool, Kahana bent down and pushed Ilima away.

At first glance Kahana's mind couldn't make sense of what his eyes saw. It was small, very small, with two arms, two legs, and a mouth that was no longer crying. Its eyes were scrunched closed against the bright sun, and part of the umbilical cord was still attached to its bellybutton.

"A boy? A newborn boy, naked, no blanket, no diaper, all alone out here? Can't be more than a day old, maybe only a few hours! Good thing it never rained last night!" Ilima nudged closer. "Enough, Ilima! Your licking will give the baby a rash!"

Ilima danced around Kahana's feet.

Kahana dropped his fishing gear, gently lifted the baby off the hard lava rock, and wrapped it securely in his towel.

You forget how small they are until you hold one again.

Ilima whimpered and nuzzled the small bundle.

"I know, I know, he looks a little gray. I think he's cold and salt's no good for a baby's skin. Look how rough and chapped it is. No, Ilima, no more licking! Eh, Lassie-wanna-be, you want to be useful, go find this baby's mama."

From the far fingertips on the deep ocean side of the

lava outcrop to the coconut trees on the shore, Kahana scanned the beach in front of him. For miles he could see it was empty. Behind him was the ocean, above him the sky, and beneath his thin rubber soles was hard, cold lava, shiny with pockets of salt and dotted with the cast-off shells of crabs.

Wherever this kid's mother is, it's not here.

Cradling the baby against his chest, Kahana walked to the last sliver of land at Piko Point and stared down into the dark blue water of the open ocean. Below the surface, shadows crawled and darting streaks of silvery light flashed, but there was no towel on the rocks, no t-shirt, no shoes, nothing. It didn't make sense.

Deep water. I bet it drops 500 feet or more, and late last night the current ran out to sea.

"Eh, Ilima, you think this baby's mama jumped in the ocean? The baby squirmed and kicked. Kahana wrapped him tighter, tucking the end of the towel under his toes. "I bet this little one's mama is one of those new age nuts. She has the baby all alone in the dark, jumps in for a swim, and ends up shark bait. Maybe that's why Kalei's hanging around. You think, Ilima?"

Ilima sniffed around the biggest saltwater pool, then sat down and whimpered. She looked back to Keikikai beach and pulled her ears tight against her head.

"You're right, Kalei didn't come through the open tunnel under Piko Point and into this pool." He lifted his chin toward the deep water. "Whatever happened, happened out there."

He looked down at the baby.

"I dunno where or who your people are, little one. Your skin is kinda gray, but not European fair. Your hair is so dark and curly, I bet you have some Hawaiian or Samoan or African blood."

Kahana's eyes traveled over the horizon in all directions, searching for anything, any clue that might lead to the baby's mother. He turned slowly, sweeping his eyes over the beach again and again, back over the rocks, and out to sea.

Nothing. Can't leave him here.

He gripped a slippah tight with his toes and stepped over a puddle. "Well, whatever. Don't worry, brah. Uncle Kahana is going to help you."

Tucking the baby into the crook of his arm and hitching up his shorts, Kahana left his fishing gear on the rocks and headed back to the beach. Tail high, Ilima scouted the way. Nestled in the towel, the baby began to warm enough to complain.

He's hungry and I don't have any milk.

Wiping his pinky on his shirt, he slipped his finger between the baby's lips. "Shhh, here," he cooed, "suck on this until we can find you something better. I know it's not what you—ouch!" Snatching his finger from the baby's mouth, he examined the small slice across the tip. "Ho! Kid, what did you do to my finger? Ilima, look!"

Ilima glanced back and yipped.

"You have a tooth, hah, little one?" Kahana gingerly brushed it with his finger. "It's sharp!" he said.

Annoyed and hungry, the baby fussed.

"I know. You want milk. I'm hurrying as fast as I can." As awkward as a tourist dancing hula, Kahana dipped and swayed, rocking the baby as he moved off the lava and onto the sand.

Like driftwood caught in an eddy, the thoughts churned through his mind.

A baby abandoned on a reef. A tooth. Niuhi shark circling. Fair skin. Dark curly hair.

At the edge of the pavilion, it clicked. "Ilima, Tutu told me that sometimes babies are born with teeth. Her sister, Aunty Lei, was born with one. Grandma said...she said... ah, no way, this can't be!"

Ilima chuffed.

Kahana gently rolled the baby over and found the mark nestled between the baby's shoulder blades, a tiny blue-black birthmark in the shape of an upside down triangle.

Eyes wide with recognition, Kahana leaned down, touched the baby nose to nose, and gently inhaled the baby's breath, filling his lungs deep. He cleared his throat. "Aloha, Cousin. I, Kahana Kaulupali, greet you as ohana."

The baby wrinkled his nose and sneezed. He grunted and turned his head, rooting for what he couldn't find. When his fist brushed his face, he latched on to it, sucking ferociously.

At least he knows enough not to bite everything that goes into his mouth.

Kahana sighed. "I know what you want, but it's not here. But don't worry, Junior-boy, everything's going to be all right now. Uncle Kahana knows exactly what to do."

He looked inland toward the mountains. "Two days ago, my niece Liz gave birth to a son. What's one more? You'll be a Westin, not a Kaulupali, but I promise they'll love you. You'll be safe there."

Leaving the sand near the big ironwood tree, Kahana, Ilima, and the baby crossed the road and headed mauka toward the Westin home, a small green plantation house tucked behind a hibiscus hedge.

4
YAWN

~ohana nui: everyone considered family whether related to you by blood, marriage, or friendship.~

I couldn't help myself. I tried to hide it behind my hand, but Uncle Kahana spotted it right away.

"I'm boring you, Z-boy?" he asked. "My old man stories too dull, hah?" He shook his head.

"It's not like that, Uncle Kahana."

"That's the problem with the younger generation. You guys don't listen."

"I'm listening," I said.

"No," he said. "You're only hearing the words I say." Uncle Kahana got up from his chair to rummage in a cupboard.

Whatever, I thought. *Uncle Kahana and Ilima found me on the reef at Piko Point and brought me to my new family. The same story a million times.*

Ilima looked up at me with her big brown eyes and batted her eyelashes. When Uncle Kahana started talking, I'd stopped petting. I put my hand on her head again and started scratching behind her ears. She sighed and settled deeper. I breathed in the scent of sun-warm dog, salt, and something that reminded me of sandalwood that I only smelled when I was around Uncle Kahana. The couch was soft, and with the pillows piled around me, I finally felt safe enough to relax.

"Here."

I opened my eyes, smelling the bag of sweet teriyaki turkey jerky before I saw it. Uncle Kahana shook it at me.

"You need to eat. I can tell. You're going white around your lips." He shook the bag again. "Here."

I reached in and grabbed a handful. "Thanks," I said. The pieces were thick and chewy, just the way I liked them. I could feel the strength start to flow from my core all the way to my fingers and toes.

"Better?"

I nodded, still chewing.

"Hear me now, Alexander Kaonakai Westin. I knew who you were the moment I found you. I brought you—"

Ilima perked her ears and chuffed.

"—Ilima and I brought you to my niece Liz and her family not because she'd just had a baby—"

"Jay," I said.

"And not because Liz and Paul had already adopted a child."

"My sister, Lilinoe."

Uncle Kahana nodded. "I took you there not because of Jay, not because of Lili, but because you were already a part of our ohana nui."

I tilted my head to the side, considering. "You told me

that I was from the part of your family that moved away from here, from Lauele down to Hohonukai a long time ago."

"Yes."

"Hohonukai, Oahu, right?"

He narrowed his eyes at me, sensing the trap. "That's right."

"Then how come I can't find Hohonukai on any map?"

"Probably because you have the wrong kind of map." He sighed. "It's because of the promises we made not to tell. That's why I can't just take you there. It's all part of what I saw and what my tutu wahine told me back in my hanabata days. My Grandmother Kaulupali's sister-in-law was—"

"Great-great-great Aunty Lei from Hohonukai. I know, I know." I sighed, frustrated. "Uncle Kahana, you told me plenny times already, fo'days. Aunty Lei was allergic to water, like me. She couldn't eat rare red meat or raw seafood like sashimi. She had to bathe using coconut oil and raw cane sugar, mixing it into a paste and rubbing it into her skin. She used coconut shells and husks to scrape off the dirt and dead skin. Tell me, Uncle Kahana, you think that made her smell like a macaroon? That's what the kids say about me, that I smell like a cookie." I looked down, picking at an imaginary burr in Ilima's coat.

I felt the warmth of Uncle Kahana's body as he leaned close to me and drew in a lungful of air. He held it for a moment, considering, then stepped back, letting it all out in a rush.

"Did you just *sniff* me?"

"Ae," he said. "No worries. You don't smell like a cookie."

"I don't?" I lifted my wrist to my nose and sniffed.

Dog. Teriyaki turkey jerky. A faint whiff of coconut oil and sugar. Nothing so strong that anyone would notice but me.

"No, you smell just like Aunty Lei. Salty and clean like the deep ocean. It's the same as the taste I get in the back of my throat when I break the surface after a long dive. Salty, with a little cleansing burn."

"How can that be?" I sniffed again, but nothing changed. "What a joke. Two people allergic to water who smell like the sea."

Uncle Kahana shrugged. "Could be worse."

"How?"

"You could smell like rotten fish."

"I'm a freak."

Ilima whined and sat up, trying to lick my face. I ignored her, staring up at Uncle Kahana, waiting for him to blink.

Meeting my stare, he flinched, although he tried to hide it. People don't like it when I look directly into their eyes. For some reason it makes them nervous and they start to fidget, looking everywhere but at me.

Uncle Kahana dropped his head and fiddled with the jerky bag. "You're not a freak," he finally said. "And Aunty Lei wasn't a freak either." He walked back to the kitchen, put the jerky away, and picked up his soda again. He took a swig, then leaned on the breakfast counter.

"What do you want to happen, Zader?"

I blinked.

"Fo'real," he said. "What do you want to happen now?"

"I don't want Alika-dem to pick on me," I said.

"Okay, we can do something about that."

"And I don't want them calling me devil or freak."

Uncle Kahana nodded. "I understand. But that's harder."

"Why?"

"Easy to make people leave you alone. Harder to make them friends."

"Then how are you going to keep them from picking on me?" I asked.

Uncle Kahana looked up from his soda can, surprised. "Me? I'm not doing anything. You're doing it."

"Me? How?"

"Pohaku was right. I gotta teach you. You and Jay. Starting next week Saturday. Both of you come to my house after dinner."

"Why not tonight?"

"Because, niele child, I need to get things ready. We'll start training Saturday."

"Training? In what?"

"Lua. The art of Hawaiian self-defense."

5

ONE SPECIAL KINE STUPID

~Blalah: a tough guy's tough guy; a moke's moke.~

Jay was already home when I got back from Uncle Kahana's. "You left your umbrella," he said, tossing it to me. "Where've you been? I went by the pavilion, the park, and Hari's, but you weren't there!"

"Uncle Kahana's."

"Why?"

"He saw me walking without a shirt. He made me come to his house and tell him what happened."

"Is he going to tell Mom?"

I shook my head. "I don't think so."

"He's going to tell and I'm going to get lickings for fighting!" Jay moaned. "What did he say when you told him I broke Alika's nose?"

I thought about it for minute, then shrugged. "He just said he wants us to come to his house Saturday."

"Why?" wailed Jay. "Is *he* going to give us lickings? Stupid head Alika! It's all his fault. I swear, Zader, when I saw those blisters on you, I lost it. You think Uncle Kahana's plenny huhu?"

"All he said was he was going to teach us Lua," I said.

"Who's going to teach you Lua?" said a voice behind me. I turned to see Char Siu on the lanai, peeking in through the screen door. "Hah? Who knows Lua?"

"Char Siu! Don't you have some Barbies to play with?" Jay said.

She stepped out of her slippahs and pushed open the door. "I came to see if Zader was okay."

"He's fine. You can go home now," Jay said.

"I never said I came to see you, Jay. I said I came to see Zader. Who knows Lua?" Char Siu was relentless when she got something in her head, especially if she thought it was a secret.

"Uncle Kahana," I said. "But what's Lua?"

Char Siu's eyes bugged out. "You're kidding, right?"

"No," I said.

Jay shrugged.

"Lua is like Hawaiian kung-fu only better! The old-time Lua masters were unreal. They could walk through walls. They could kill with their thoughts!" Char Siu hopped up and down, bobbing and weaving like a mynah bird. "They could strike faster than an eel after fish. They could break thigh bones with only their pinkies!" She held hers up for inspection.

Jay snorted. "No way. I think you been watching too many cartoons."

"Lua is real! The reason you never heard about it is because it's secret! My brothers told me their kung-fu sifu told them that all the old Hawaiian chiefs and their body-guards knew Lua. They're like the delta-ninja-warrior forces of old Hawaii." She turned to me. "Zader, you think Uncle Kahana would teach me, too?"

"As if!" said Jay. "Like Uncle Kahana knows Lua! He probably just watched too many Jackie Chan movies."

"I dunno know, Jay," I said. "Uncle Kahana knows a lot of old-kine stuffs."

"My mom told me long ago there were wahine Lua warriors," said Char Siu.

"Shibai! Like a girl can be a warrior!" Jay sneered.

"Fo'real! Kamehameha the Great had hundreds of female Lua warriors in his army on the Big Island. Plus my mother told me the women of Kauai were famous for their ability to use cords to trip and strangle people."

"Psshtt. Cords. More like jump ropes. Girls can't be warriors," said Jay.

"What, Jay, you want me to show you what a girl warrior can do?" Char Siu shook her fist at him. "Like beef?"

"I think we've had all the fighting we can handle today, Char Siu."

We all jumped and spun towards the kitchen where Mom was standing at the doorway. She'd come in the back-door while we were arguing. She tossed her purse and keys on the coffee table and walked over to me. "Let me see," she said.

I held out my arms and rotated as she poked and prodded, brushing a sore spot here and there with her fingertips, examining every square inch of my face, shoulders, and back. I felt her fingers linger on my birthmark, that odd triangle between my shoulders usually hidden by a t-shirt.

It's just a giant freckle, exactly like what Becky has all over her face. Why'd they have to make a big deal out of it?

Mom sighed, then pressed a dry kiss on my forehead. "Doesn't look too bad. When Mrs. Kanahele called me at work—"

"Alika's grandma called you?" Jay said.

"Uh, I gotta go," Char Siu said. "I think I hear my mom calling me to go wash the rice." She slipped out the door and was down the steps faster than a cockaroach under the stove when the kitchen lights flipped on.

"Laters," I hollered. She waved without turning, heading down the driveway and across the street to her house.

"She called me," Mom said, "to tell me Jay broke Alika's nose."

"What did you say?" I asked, giving Jay side-eye. We both braced for the explosion.

"I said, good thing I wasn't there. I would've broken Alika's neck." Mom reached up and tucked some hair behind her ear.

Our eyes bugged out.

Did Mom just say she would've broken Alika's neck?

"What?" She looked at us. "Close your mouths. You look like a couple of bufos."

"So . . . we're not in trouble, then?" Jay asked.

"I don't like fighting, Jay. But throwing water on Zader

wasn't like name calling or playground pushing. It could've been deadly. Alika has to learn he can't do that."

"You think he learned his lesson?" I asked.

Mom reached out and tousled my hair. "I hope so. But Alika's one special kine stupid, less to do with IQ than the need to be the biggest, baddest blalah around. Jay's punch should have taught him to think twice before he tries anything with you again. Because if you mess with the Westin boys—"

"Jay's going bust your nose." I play-punched Jay in the shoulder.

"No act," he said, but he was grinning.

6
DREAMS AND WISHES

~Hanai: adopted; to adopt; to love and cherish as your own.~

"**T**his is the place I was telling you about, Zader. We have to be careful now," said Dream Girl. We were kneeling behind a tower carved out of rough stone. She stood and peeked around the corner, then motioned me to stand. "Ready to fly?" she asked. I nodded and pushed off, effortlessly rising near the tower's peak to hover behind a rampart. Below us was a medieval courtyard. People in brightly colored clothes were scurrying in and out of doors and through archways, carrying chests and baskets full of things I couldn't identify, but somehow knew were very valuable. I glanced at Dream Girl. Her long, dark hair swirled and twisted in the breeze; she kept pushing it out of her face. I reached into my pocket and handed her a piece of string.

"Thanks," she said. "You're lucky your hair is short." She gathered her hair into a quick ponytail and secured it with the string. "In fact, you're very lucky to be you." I nodded, not knowing why this was true, only that it was.

From below, trumpets sounded a fanfare. I should have

been startled, but wasn't. I felt a little detached from everything, as if I were drugged and watching from behind a wall of glass instead of floating beside Dream Girl in the air. I could feel the cool breeze as it flowed along my face and through my hair. It had an odd taste to it, metallic and bitter. I pinched myself and saw the mark it raised on my arm. I shook my head to clear it.

In the courtyard people poured out of the doorways and quickly lined up on both sides of the tallest archway, the one directly in front of us. "He's coming," she said. "Don't let him see you, no matter what." A thrill shot through me, straight from my gut to my brain. I was going to see him again, the man who inspired terror and awe.

I saw his shadow first as it entered the courtyard before him. It was long, far longer than any I'd seen below. Next, his bare feet appeared—minus a big toe, I noted. It gave him a slight limp, a rolling awkwardness and abruptness when he moved that startled. His shins and thighs followed, then a narrow waist and broad shoulders, and finally, his face framed by black shoulder-length hair shot through with strands of silver. He stood in the archway, massive and powerful, utterly confident in himself. Only his eyes moved, back and forth, searching the faces before him. I knew he was looking for me. Before I could lower my head below the rampart's edge, our eyes met—his eyes were dark, flat, relentless. And mine were simply . . . open. As if from far away, I heard Dream Girl whimper as I watched the man parted his lips, revealing too long, too sharp teeth. I drew a breath to scream—

"Zader! Zader!" a harsh whisper in my ear. I opened my eyes. Jay was leaning over me, his hand on my shoulder, shaking. "You awake?"

"Yeah," I croaked. "Thanks."

"You were having that dream again. You were thrashing and moaning."

"Sorry."

"You've been having them a lot."

"Not really," I hedged.

"Twice this week," said Jay. "Last Sunday and now today."

Last night when I was clearing the dishes, I lifted a bone from Dad's plate. There was a little bit of meat clinging to it, red in the middle and looking so good I couldn't help myself. I nibbled along the bone, the meat tender and juicy, the flavor slipping over my tongue and down my throat in a thick, rich cloak of awesomeness. It was much better than my charred and dried-out piece, so much better that I had to wonder if my steak was even beef at all.

I thought back. Last Sunday, Aunty Amy brought over some sushi with crab meat rolled inside. My allergies again, but this time instead of blisters they gave me wild dreams about a friend I called Dream Girl.

I liked being with Dream Girl. In my allergy dreams Dream Girl and I did crazy things like fly and chase each other through fields of grasses and trees I'd never seen in real life. Those kinds of dreams I liked, but sometimes the dreams made me afraid. There was a dark shadow figure, a man we sometimes spied on, a man with too many teeth, who never did anything to us but made us deeply afraid. I was scared for no reason I could see, except that whatever scary thing was out there, Dream Girl was frightened, too.

"I woke you?" I sat up and rubbed my face. My head hurt a little and my nose felt pinched and sore. I sniffed and thought for a moment I'd caught a lingering metallic scent, like when Dad used the soldering iron. I cautiously sniffed again, but it was gone.

Jay stood up. "Nah. I was getting up now anyways."

The light coming through our windows was very pale. The sun was not up yet, but would be soon. I watched Jay make his bed. "Going surfing?"

"Yeah."

"Early, yeah?"

"That's when the waves are best."

"Meeting Frankie?"

Jay grabbed a t-shirt off the floor. Through the shirt he mumbled, "Later. He won't surf before dawn, the panty. He comes an hour or two after sunrise. He says his mother makes him do chores, but I know the truth. He's scared of sharks."

I thought about what I knew about sharks and decided Frankie had a point. "They come in at night to feed, yeah? In close to shore." I said.

"So they say." Jay picked up the sunscreen from under the dresser.

I cocked my head at him. "You're not afraid?"

"No."

"No?"

"No. Terrified," Jay confessed.

"You ever seen a shark? I mean, out there, surfing?" I asked.

"Couple times." He paused, sunscreen white on his nose. "Plenny times. I've seen them along the reef bottom, cruising out by first breaks at Nalupuki."

"Fo'real?" I asked.

"Yeah, fo'real."

"How big?"

"Small. Baby kine. Around two or three feet, mostly black tip reef. There's one out there I've seen four or five times that's huge, about nine feet, longer than me on my board." Jay shrugged. "But most aren't big."

"Big enough."

He nodded. "Once when I dove under a wave, I saw one out in the distance, a hammerhead. Had to be twelve, maybe fourteen feet." He shook his head. "That time I got out."

I watched him take an old beach towel from the back of our door and toss it over his shoulder. "Why?" I asked. "If you know they're there, why surf at all?"

Jay turned to me, chewing on his bottom lip, choosing his words carefully. "Don't tell Mom, okay? But one time, I was hanging out with some seagulls, just floating out past first breaks when I saw a shark go after a bird. The bugger was so fast! He hit the bird and swallowed it before the bird even knew it was coming. I was sitting on my board not fifteen feet away. He'd rather have a mouthful of feathers than a chunk out of me. That's when I knew." His eyes held mine. "I knew then that it didn't matter if I was surfing in the early dawn or high noon, in shallow water or deep, by myself or with choke guys. If a shark wanted me, it would have me. There's nothing I can do, except stay out of the water. And I can't do that." He looked down. "If I can't do anything, waste time being scared, yeah? And I don't want to waste time when the waves are pumping. Besides, everybody knows sharks only like white meat. Good thing I'm tan." He grinned and opened our bedroom door.

"Jay," I said.

"Yeah?"

"Be careful, yeah?"

"Always, brah, always."

I heard Jay close the front door and grab his board off the front lanai. I sat there thinking about what he'd said. I reached under my bed and pulled out my sketchbook and art supplies, a cigar box of random pens, chalk, charcoal, and pencils.

In the box was a shark tooth on a leather cord, part of a small package I'd received on my seventh birthday. Mom said I'd gotten a package every year on my birthday since I turned one. This year she and Dad decided I was old enough to open it myself. She didn't let me keep the natural Tahitian pearl the size and shape of a glass eye; it was too valuable to leave it hanging around the house.

Earlier this summer, the week after my eleventh birthday, Mom took me to Bank of Hawaii in Honolulu and showed me the security box that held the previous ten birthday gifts, plus one inexplicable one. Alone with Mom in the client room, I opened the large metal box. I hesitated a moment, just looking at everything sitting on the padded velvet bottom, shining softy in the fluorescent lights.

"Go on," said Mom. "You can pick them up. They're yours."

"I feel like I should be wearing white gloves or something," I said.

Mom laughed. "I'm pretty sure you aren't going to break anything if you pick it up."

All together in the box against the black velvet, they were overwhelming; they didn't seem real, more like something from Long's at Halloween, plastic booty for a pretend pirate's treasure chest.

I held each of the eleven previous gifts in my hand for a moment, trying to get a sense of the person who sent them: a small 24k gold bar stamped with Chinese characters; gold cuff links set with square-cut rubies the size of Jolly Ranchers; a thick silvery chain Mom said was platinum with a large floral pendant made of thumbnail-sized rose-cut diamonds and smaller sapphires, rubies, and emeralds; a ceremonial Peruvian mask of gold inlaid with obsidian and jade; a twenty-five-inch double strand of perfectly matched ten millimeter natural white Hanadama Akoya pearls; a jade statue of a Chinese warrior on a rearing horse the color and opacity of green sea glass; a gold cup called a chalice with a hammered design of interlinking blocks along the edge; an African ivory flute with ebony and opal inlay; a twenty-inch necklace made of black, red, and gold dolphins carved from coral, each link joined by 24k gold waves; a short dagger with a jeweled hilt in the shape of a leaping jaguar.

Lastly, tucked in the back of the box, was one that didn't seem to belong with the others. I picked up the odd gift—number eleven—which didn't make sense if I received one each year. There should be ten gifts, with the new Tahitian pearl for eleven. I turned it around and around in my hands, weaving the leather cord through my fingers. It was a good-sized shark's tooth, about the size of a quarter, wrapped at the top with a twist of copper wire, and strung on cheap rawhide cord dyed black. It was the kind of thing popular in Waikiki tourist traps. It didn't belong in a pirate's chest.

"You got that on your seventh birthday. It was tucked inside the flute. It fell out when I picked it up," Mom said.

"What do you think it means?"

"I don't know," she said. "Probably nothing. Most likely it got mixed in during shipping. All of the other gifts were wrapped in ti or banana leaves. This one was in an old box."

"Or maybe somebody goofing around saw the flute and dropped it in as a joke?"

"Maybe," she said.

"Can I keep it? Just this one. It's not valuable like the rest."

Mom thought about it. "Sure. I don't see why not."

I carefully coiled the cord and placed the shark tooth necklace in my pocket. We tuck in the eleventh gift, this year's Tahitian pearl, and closed up the security box, left the bank, and went to Zippy's for lunch.

Sitting in a booth near the back, I blew on my chili and rice while Mom opened her bento. "Who sends me the gifts, Mom?"

She unwrapped her chopsticks and cracked them apart, thinking. "I don't know," she said. "Not for sure. I think they come from your birth family—at least that's what Uncle Kahana tells me." I opened my mouth to speak, but she cut me off with a wave of her chopsticks. "Somebody not related to you acts as a go-between. He gives the gifts to Uncle Kahana just before your birthday. Uncle says he's never spoken directly with your—" She swallowed. "Your other mother."

I scooped up a bit of chili and rice. "That bugs you, yeah?"

"No." She picked up a piece of teri beef, then put it down. "Yeah, it does. I don't want to share you, Zader. People call you our hanai son, but that's a distinction your Dad and I don't see. Hanai, adopted, is just a word. You're my son."

I thought about my other family out there somewhere. I must have a dad and a mom, aunties, uncles, cousins, grandparents—maybe even a brother or sister. I shook my head. "You're my mom," I said. "Period. Forget about hanai. I don't want to be shared."

Mom laughed and ate a bite of fish. "Those things they sent are valuable. You can use them to pay for college, buy a house, start a business. As much as I'd rather you didn't have another family, I have to admit they've made it so you can buy anything you'll ever want."

"Like an airplane or Lamborghini?"

She laughed again. "I said they're yours and they are, but I'm going to keep them for you a little longer, just until you're out of the hot rod phase." My face fell. "You'll thank me later," she said.

"Doubt it."

I put away that memory as I pulled the cord through my fingers, wondering about the fingers that selected and attached the shark's tooth.

They're rich, I thought. *They own jewelry stores or art museums. They travel the world buying masterpieces for souvenirs.*

Or maybe they're not buying souvenirs; they're actually archaeologists, like Indiana Jones. That's a dangerous life—headhunters and snakes and Nazis; too dangerous for a kid.

Or maybe they're in the witness protection program, hiding from the Yakuza. That fits. The Yakuza's hard core; they wipe out everyone from the oldest to the youngest—ending the line forever. They had to hide me away so I could continue the family line in secret. Even though they can't acknowledge me, they're sending me these things, my birthright, one piece at a time; they don't want the Yakuza to know I'm alive!

Or maybe it's the other way around. My birth mother is the daughter of a Yakuza crime lord! She gave me away to hide me from her father! Her father didn't approve of my father! My birth mother is sending me things that her father wouldn't miss!

I sighed. *Whatever. They didn't want me. Their loss. I'm glad my real family found me. If I ever do meet them, I'm giving them back all their stuff.*

I started to put the shark tooth away in my art box, but I paused, considering. I took the cord and placed it around my neck, the shark tooth surprisingly heavy against my chest. As I leaned forward to flip the sketchbook's page, the tooth gently thumped against my chest, a second heartbeat to my own. *It's in the way*, I thought, slipping it under the collar of my shirt. It settled there, rough and warm against my skin.

Looking back at me from the pages of my sketchbook was another image from my recurring nightmare. In my picture, Dream Girl was standing on cobblestones in front of a building that curved and bent like it grew from the ground up. You could see her from the back, her long hair and old-fashioned cape billowing in the wind. The door to the building was partially open. In the gloom, a person stood just to the side of the doorway. You couldn't see the face, just the impression of eyes, nose, and mouth. I'd sketched it with pencil and then inked over it in black pen. I studied it for a moment and decided it needed color. I chose a red oil crayon and started on Dream Girl's cape.

After a while, the image blurred and changed, the red running off the paper and bleeding onto the bed. A sudden shock of coldness, and I was no longer in my bed but under a glass dome looking up at the sky. The sunlight was weak, as if the glass were tinted, and odd shadows rippled along the sand floor. In front of me was a long sand dune, and I began walking, trudging through the sand, my footprints mushy and indistinct. As I climbed the dune, the sunlight got brighter; I kept my eye on the sun as I walked until I saw the bottom of Jay's surfboard, his feet dangling over the sides, flying too high in the air above me, too high and too close to the sun. I marveled he didn't burn to a crisp. I gathered myself, then jumped, powerful and strong, flew like an arrow to his board, and sank my teeth into Jay's leg, crunching through flesh and tendon and bone. Hot, sticky blood flooded my mouth, its scent rich and thick in my nose, sliding down my throat, coating it like fine melted chocolate.

Delicious.

With a jerk and a moan, for the second time that morning, I woke up from a nightmare.

1
BALANCE

~Huna na mea huna: keep secret that which is sacred.~

"Zader and Jay, plus one," mused Uncle Kahana when we showed up at his door. "I should have figured you'd be here, Char Siu."

"Uncle Kahana, tell her," said Jay.

"Tell her what?" asked Uncle Kahana.

"Tell her—"

"Uncle Kahana," interrupted Char Siu, "can a girl be a Lua warrior?"

"Of course," said Uncle Kahana.

"Nyah!" said Char Siu, sticking her tongue out at Jay.

"What!"

"Come in, come in! We don't stand in the open discussing sacred things!" scolded Uncle Kahana. We took off our slippahs and shuffled in, greeting Ilima while Uncle Kahana shut the door. "Now," he said, rubbing his hands together, "if, and I mean if, I decide to accept you as haumana, my students, in our pa lua, our Lua school, we're gonna have to get a few things straight."

I looked around the apartment. Uncle Kahana had

pushed the kitchen table to the far right and stacked the coffee table and chairs upside down on top of it. The bare wooden floor stretched from end to end.

It looks like a basketball gym, I thought.

Uncle Kahana flapped his hand at us, motioning us to sit on the floor facing him on the couch. Ilima padded over to her pillow, tucked out of the way under the kitchen table.

He considered each of us in turn, waiting until the wiggles were out, our legs crossed and hands loosely clasped in our laps. We waited, excited but respectful.

Finally he nodded. "Maikaʻi," he muttered. "Good. We begin. Lua is not about fighting. It's about balance."

"Why?" Char Siu asked.

"So you don't fall when you punch," Jay said.

Uncle Kahana sighed and rubbed his chin. "Stand up, Jay."

Oh-oh, I thought.

Jay scrambled to his feet, eager. "How do you want me to stand?"

"On one foot. Balance."

Jay stood there, strong on one leg, not twitching or shaking. Char Siu and I just sat there, watching. After a moment or two Uncle Kahana walked to the kitchen and got the broom out of the closet. "Here," he said, handing it to Jay, "hold this over your head. Balance."

"Okay," Jay said.

I could never do that.

"Lua," said Uncle Kahana, "requires three things: perseverance, acceptance, and pursuit." He held up a finger.

"First, perseverance. You have to work hard, persist, and practice so that the heart, mind, and spirit function as one. This idea is called hoʻomau." He paused. "How you doing, Jay?"

"Fine."

"Maikaʻi." Uncle Kahana walked to the shelves and picked up a book. He carefully placed the book on Jay's head. "Balance," he said.

"Mmmmph," said Jay.

Two more minutes, tops.

Uncle Kahana turned back to Char Siu and me and held up a second finger. "Number two: acceptance. This means understanding how energy flows throughout the universe and striving to work with it, not against it. This idea is called nalu, same as the word for ocean waves. You like to surf, Jay?"

"Yeah. Whoa." Jay teetered a little, releasing one hand from the broom to clamp the book back on his head.

"Balance, Jay."

"Okay."

"Both hands on the broom."

"Okay."

"Now, Zader, you don't know this like Jay does, but when the wave comes you have to relax into it. No way you can make the wave change what it's going to do. It's better to try to understand the wave and choose your moment to leave. You got it?"

"Go with the flow," I said.

"Maikaʻi," said Uncle Kahana. "Still okay, Jay?"

"Mmmmph," said Jay.

"He looks kinda wobbly," said Char Siu.

"Mmmmph," said Jay.

"Hold the broom higher."

Jay straightened as best he could, sweat beading down his neck.

Uncle Kahana is making a point, but I don't know what. Maybe that he's the boss?

"Lua is all about balance," Uncle Kahana continued.

"What's the last thing, Uncle?" Char Siu asked.

"Hah?"

"You said Lua had three things: ho'omau, nalu, and—"

"Ho'i hou. Pursuit of knowledge through study of the past and reflection on the present and future. Lua requires you to examine yourself, your place in the world, the reasons things happen, and the harmony among all things. Balance—"

"—I . . . I . . . help!" Jay squeaked as he crashed to the floor.

"Careful," said Uncle Kahana, "don't sweat on 'Zader!"

Gasping for breath, Jay gave Uncle Kahana stink eye and wiped his forehead on his sleeve. "No worries," he said, moving closer to Char Siu.

"Don't sweat on me either," she said, moving away.

Jay gave her double-stink eye and rubbed his face on his shirt again.

Uncle Kahana picked up the book and broom and put them away. "So, Jay, what did you learn about balance?"

"I need more practice."

Uncle Kahana's mouth dropped open and he stood there blinking like a fish. "Bwahahahaha!" he exploded, the sound bubbling up deep from his belly. Ilima barked and leapt from her pillow, running to lick Jay's face.

Char Siu and I exchanged a look, both of us clueless.

"James Kapono Westin, your parents named you well!" He snorted and rubbed his eyes. "Chee, I never laughed like that in a long time." He chortled a bit more, then flopped onto the couch; Ilima climbed on his lap.

"The highest virtue a Hawaiian can embody is pono. When something is pono, it is exactly right, it is all that is good and moral and correct. It is said to be in perfect in balance, James Kapono Westin. The fact that you understand that you need more practice before becoming Ka-pono, or the Righteous One, Jay, gives me plenny hope for you yet!"

"So . . . you gonna teach us Lua, Uncle Kahana?" asked Char Siu.

He tipped his head to the side, looking at us, his hand idly running down Ilima's back. She lifted her head and looked up at him. "Woof!"

"Think so?" said Uncle Kahana.

"Woof," Ilima said again before settling back down in his lap, closing her eyes as his hand stroked her head.

Purring?! I think that sound is Ilima purring!

"Okay. Yes, Char Siu, I accept you and the boys as haumana in our pa lua." From the couch he turned his attention to the lanai. Through the sliding glass door the sky glowed with the colors of sunset as the sun slipped into the ocean. For a moment he looked lost, a sadness in his eyes I had never seen before. Jay and I exchanged glances. Char Siu caught our eyes and shook her head. We waited.

His eyes still on the sky, Uncle Kahana spoke. "Usually, pa lua are under the direction of ʻolohe lua, someone who has been recognized as a master of Lua by other masters."

"Like a black belt?" Char Siu asked.

"Little bit." He nodded.

"Uncle, you're ʻolohe lua, right?" Jay asked.

"No."

"Why not?" I asked.

The soft orange glow through the door was warm on his face, but his presence was far, far away. "Because my ʻolohe lua, my father, never name me as such," he said to the past.

I felt Jay inhale and open his mouth. Char Siu punched his leg, shaking her head. For once, Jay closed his mouth without making a sound.

Uncle Kahana blinked, turning away from whatever memories were deep in his heart, his attention back to us. "I can't be ʻolohe lua to you, but I can be your kumu. Your teacher. As your kumu, I require two things of you this evening."

Eyes bright, Char Siu leaned forward. "Yes," she said.

"One: that all of you understand the sacred nature of what I am going to teach you. Lua is serious. It is not to be spoken of outside our pa lua. Huna na mea huna. Keep secret that which is sacred. Clear?"

"Yes, Uncle," I said.

"Say ae, Kumu,' each of you."

"Ae, Kumu," we said.

"In the past each pa lua had a password. Nobody could enter if they didn't know the password. Our password is *pono*. Say it."

"Pono," we chanted.

"Maikaʻi."

"Kumu," I said, "the second thing?"

"Put all the furniture back where it belongs."

8
Go Pro

~Shave ice: what every snow cone wants to be when it grows up.~

I watched Jay paddle out, following Nili-boy's wake to where the three to five foot waves were swelling, rising to break inside the reef at Nalupuki beach. Jay's friend, Frankie Machado, was already out there, clenching his board in a death grip and trying to look unafraid. I knew Mom would be super ticked at Jay for going surfing at Nalupuki beach, especially when she wasn't here to supervise. Jay and Frankie were hounding Nili-boy, our cousin from Waimanalo, trying to get him to teach them how to surf. I wasn't worried; it was a medium sized day at Nalupuki. Besides, I swear Nili-boy is half dolphin.

I flipped the umbrella over my head to rest on my other shoulder and twirled it. I hated it almost as much as I hated getting wet. It was a necessary evil and one of Mom's conditions if I wanted to leave the lanai. The wind was blowing off the ocean, but I was sitting on a picnic table high on the hill above the pavilion, far enough away to be safe from the salt spray. When the wind was right I could hear Nili-boy's encouragement and instructions along with Jay and

Frankie's whoops when they caught a wave and made it to the beach in one piece.

I lifted the back of the umbrella and examined the mountains behind me. The afternoon clouds were stacking up, getting ominous. If I didn't leave soon, I'd blister my feet running home in the rain. The only thing worse would be the scolding I'd get from Mom for wearing slippahs instead of shoes. I wiggled my toes.

Feet gotta breathe, right?

I was working on my sketch when the smell of blood and salt filled my nose.

"Howzit, Z-boy," Uncle Kahana said.

"Howzit, Uncle. Looks like a good size ulu." The fish was still glossy, dripping pale pink saltwater from its tail to the ground. Ilima trotted behind, nosing along a secret trail only she could see.

"Not bad. Too much for Ilima and me. I was thinking about inviting Hari over." He gestured toward the beach. "Jay surfing?"

"Yeah."

"Nalupuki side?"

"Yeah."

"Ho, Liz's gonna be mad if she finds out."

"You gonna tell Mom?"

"You think I'm stupid?" he said. "Nili-boy's out there, yeah?"

"Yeah."

"Jay's fine." We watched Jay catch a wave and held our breath as it formed a curl and swallowed Jay whole.

"Cheehooooo!" Jay shouted as he shot out the end, a bullet fired from a rifle.

"He's good," Uncle Kahana said.

"He won the last Menehune Surf Meet."

"Fo'real? The one at Pipeline?"

"Yeah. The announcer said Jay could go pro."

"No kidding?"

"Jay wants to go pro," I said.

"Good for him."

"Uncle Kahana?"

"Yeah?"

"You think Jay can go pro?"

Uncle Kahana watched the ocean for a moment, considering. Finally, he nodded. "I've seen Jay surf plenny times. He's got the talent. Takes some luck, too."

"Practice," I said.

"Plus that."

"Lots of it." I sighed.

Uncle Kahana raised an eyebrow and gave me side-eye. "What's on your mind, Z-boy?"

"Tons of water out there," I said.

He rolled his head on his shoulders, thinking about what I said. "You and Jay do everything together."

"Almost."

"Char Siu?"

"She's a girl."

He nodded, then flicked some sand off his knees. "It's not right for an island boy to be stuck on a hill."

I didn't know what to say to that, so I said nothing.

After the silence had stretched out for a bit, I opened my sketchbook and picked up my pencil. I was working on the curl of a wave when Uncle Kahana finally spoke again.

"Let me think about it a little bit. Come, Ilima, we go."

"Eh, Mary Poppins! Howzit!" A face peeked around the edge of my umbrella, hair flying hammajang in the wind.

"Char Siu, how many times do I have to tell you not to call me that?"

"I guess some more." She grinned. "I'll make it up to you. My mom paid me for pulling weeds this morning. I filled two big trash bags! So hot today, I just bought a large strawberry-lilikoʻi-guava shave ice from Hari's. Wanna bite?"

"With ice cream and li hing mui powder?"

"Of course. Mac-nut ice cream on the bottom, li hing mui on top."

"No snow cap?"

She shook her head. "Too sweet."

"Never," I said.

"You want some or not?" Char Siu held out the paper cone overflowing with red, yellow, and pink shave ice. She handed me the wooden paddle and I loaded it with red, my favorite. The shave ice shocked my tongue and the roof of my mouth and trickled down the back of my throat, tingling like a mixture of lime soda and strawberry pop rocks. My lips prickled and itched a little where ice on the paddle touched them. It was so 'ono. I dug in the mountain of shave ice for another bite.

Char Siu climbed on the table and sat next to me under the umbrella. "Good, yeah?" she said, sucking the syrup from the bottom of the paper cone with a plastic straw.

"Yeah," I said. "Makes my mouth tingle."

"Sore?"

"Nah. Worth it."

She took the plastic straw out and used the scoop on the end to shovel shave ice into her mouth. She gestured toward the ocean. "Jay surfing?"

"Yeah. Frankie and Nili-boy are out there, too."

"Nalupuki? Aunty Liz's gonna kill him," she said.

I slurped another scoop. Heaven. "Yeah," I said.

Out in the ocean Nili-boy sat on his board and motioned Jay to back up. A new set was coming in and the first wave was all Frankie's.

"Okay, watch 'em, Frankie, watch 'em! You see how it's building? Try timing it. Watch now. Ready? Go, go, go, go!" bellowed Nili-boy.

Frankie looked back at him.

"I said GO! Paddle, brah!" roared Nili-boy.

Frankie hesitated another moment, then began to slap at the water in front of the oncoming swell.

"Wait!" shrieked Nili-boy. "Too late! Bail, brah. Bail, bail, bail!" Frankie hesitated again, but instead of immediately turning into the wave and shoving hard on the front edge of his board to dive under the wave, he tried to reverse direction and float over the top. Physics and Mother Nature are unforgiving; the wave hauled him up and crashed down, rolling and rolling him in the white water, a washing machine on the spin cycle.

"Ouch," said Char Siu.

"That's gonna hurt," I said. I took another bite.

"Idiot." Char Siu snorted. "You can't run from a wave. You gotta meet it head on. Everybody knows that."

We watched as Frankie's board popped to the surface. Frankie's head broke water for a second, allowing him one soggy gasp of air before getting sucked down for spin cycle two.

"He's gonna be digging sand out fo'days," giggled Char Siu.

"Yeah."

"Jay!" yelled Nili-boy. "Just wait. I gotta go help Frankie." Effortlessly, Nili-boy nabbed the second wave, cutting to the right to maximize speed. Near the shore he spotted Frankie, waterlogged and coughing. Nili-boy smoothly pulled out of the wave and jogged over. Throwing an arm around Frankie's shoulders, he helped him to the beach.

"Brah," Nili-boy said, "Go means go! Bail means no go! You scared, you hesitate, you drown. Here. Sit. I'll find your board."

"Lucky," said Char Siu.

"Yeah," I said.

Out in the ocean, the third wave of the set—the biggest

by far—was coming in. Jay started paddling into position. Nili-boy looked out. "No!" he boomed, "Too big! Pass!"

Jay waved and started paddling and kicking with all his might. He caught the nine-foot wave near the top, shot down the face of it, tucked into the sweet spot in front of the curl, and rode it to the beach. "Cheehooooo!" he whooped, pumping his fist in the air. "That was awesome!"

Nili-boy ran up to him. "Jay! Unreal, Cuz, unreal!" They bumped fists and high-fived. Watching, I could feel Jay's thrill rush through me, the adrenalin pumping hard and fast, breath coming in gasps. And he was grinning. For a moment I was standing on the shore, white backwash swirling around my knees, Nili-boy's grip on my shoulder, solid and proud. I turned and looked toward the hill and saw myself and Char Siu sitting on a picnic table under a ridiculous umbrella.

So this is what it's like to be Jay.

I blinked. Char Siu nudged me and said, "Jay's amazing. Stupid, but amazing." She shook her head and ate the last bite.

On the beach Frankie coughed some more and hung his head, nose dripping into the sand. Jay and Nili-boy walked over, dropped their boards beside him, and sat down, talking.

Char Siu crushed the paper cone and tossed it in the rubbish can. I threw the wooden paddle and missed. "Panty," Char Siu said. When I started to get up, she put her hand on my leg, pushing down. "Nah," she said, "I'll get it." She jumped off, picked up the shave ice paddle, and tossed it into the trash. That's when she saw my new kite, hidden in the shadows under the table. "Wow, Zader!" she said, eyes wide. "That's yours?"

"Yeah."

"For your birthday?"

"Yeah." I pointed with my chin. "Jay got a surfboard."

"Can see?" I nodded, and she carefully brought it out from under the table, making sure the tips didn't bend or scratch. "Small." Char Siu turned it over and held it up to the sun. "One quarter-Hawaiian?" she asked.

"Yeah. Uncle Kahana knows a guy who custom made it for me." Even a half-sized Hawaiian stunt kite was too much for any eleven-year-old. In a strong breeze, a half-Hawaiian would lift me right off the ground. I imagined what that would be like, sailing through the clouds, over the pali cliffs, all the way to the sun. "Uncle Kahana said its name was Iolani, and if I respected it, it would soar like a hawk, but always return to me."

"Gorgeous," she said.

"Yeah."

"Why aren't you flying it? Get plenny wind."

I shrugged. "Can if you like."

Char Siu's eyes bugged out. "Fo'real?" she breathed.

"Shoots. I'll hold the handles and you run out and launch it."

I put down my umbrella and shook out the lines. It took

us a couple of tries to get Iolani up and soaring. The double lines that allowed it to do spectacular stunts kept crossing, but once up, Iolani stretched its blue and black wings wide and rose with the wind.

Beautiful.

Char Siu ran back to me. "Ho, Zader, it's awesome!"

"Yeah!"

"Can you do any stunts?"

"Uncle Kahana taught me a few things." I gauged the wind, then pulled on the right handle. Iolani swooped straight down then soared back up when I evened the lines.

"Wow!" said Char Siu.

"Watch," I said. By pulling and releasing the two lines, I made the kite swoop, spin, dive, and cut through the sky in an aerial dance to the music in my head. Char Siu oo'ed and ah'ed like it was the Fourth of July. I gave her side-eye.

"Wanna try?"

"You sure?" she gasped.

"Take this handle. Now the other . . . you got it." Iolani wobbled a little, then found its rhythm again, diving and swooping, dancing to new music. Char Siu's grin was bigger than her face.

When I went back to the table to pick up my umbrella, I saw Mrs. Machado's truck pull up to the pavilion, bass rumbling and girls hanging out the windows and lounging in the back. It looked like it was her turn to drive the hula halau home. I turned and saw Jay and Frankie at the

showers, rinsing off the sand and salt. Nili-boy was back in the ocean, heading out to the bigger waves over Nalupuki reef. If they were lucky, Mrs. Machado would think Jay and Frankie had been at Keikikai all afternoon.

"Eh, Jay," said Frankie, "You wanna sleep over? My mom said you can."

The wind was blowing their conversation right to me, as clearly as if I were standing next to them. Mom called it bat ears. I just thought everyone talked too loud.

"Sure." Jay looked over to the hill. I waved. "What about Zader? Can he come, too?"

Frankie looked down, shaking the sand off his slippahs. "I dunno. I can ask."

It's not about me, I thought. *It's Frankie's mother.*

Mrs. Machado planned everything in advance. She even made a calendar of dinners one month ahead. It didn't matter if the ahi looked junk and pork chops were on sale; if the calendar said ahi for dinner, she bought the ahi.

Frankie picked up his board, threw his towel over his shoulder, and headed to the truck. Mrs. Machado's elbow was hanging out her window. "Good fun?" she asked.

"Yeah."

"Do I need to take Jay home first so he can change?" Frankie fidgeted, pulling at his wet trunks. Mrs. Machado's eyes narrowed. "What? He can't come?"

"Yeah, he can, but . . ."

"But what?"

Looking at the ground Frankie mumbled, "Can Zader

come, too? If Zader can't, then I think Jay's not going to come."

Mrs. Machado's eyes narrowed more. "We already talked about that." Frankie glanced toward the showers where Jay was waiting, wiping down his board, taking his time. "You know how I feel about that kid. Your sister Punkin doesn't like him either."

"Zader's okay," said Frankie, almost too softly to hear.

"He has all these allergy rules. I never know what he can or can't eat. And water? That kid must be so stink; he never bathes."

"Zader doesn't stink, Mrs. Machado," piped Mele from the back seat. "He bathes with coconut oil. He smells kinda sweet. Like fresh roasted macadamias."

I touched my nose to my shoulder and sniffed. Nothing. Not sweet, not stink, just . . . me.

"And where am I going get that much coconut oil? That stuff is ex-*pan*-sive. What do you think, coconut oil grows on trees?" complained Mrs. Machado.

Uh, yeah, it does, stupid head, I thought. *Plus one small bottle lasts more than a week. It's not like I fill a bathtub!*

Char Siu was saying something about clouds, but I tuned her out. Jay started walking slowly across the grass to the pickup.

"Zader has creepy eyes," said Punkin, "so dark you can't see the pupils." She shuddered. "It freaks me out."

"Yeah," said Trudy. "They look blank, but they're always watching."

Hah? What was I supposed to do? Walk around with my eyes closed?

"And that umbrella. Everywhere he goes, he drags that umbrella. Like it's gonna rain any minute," sneered Punkin.

Frankie just stood there, looking at his feet. His mother said, "No. Zader cannot come over. If that means Jay won't, then fine."

Jay reached the sidewalk. "Aloha, Mrs. Machado," he called.

"Howzit, Jay. Good fun?"

He crossed the asphalt to the truck's window. "Oh, yeah, Mrs. Machado. Nice waves."

Through the windshield Mrs. Machado looked at the ocean off Keikikai Beach. Flat, flat, flat, more flat than wonton wrappers, more flat than glass. Off Nalupuki she could see the waves had picked up, now a consistent five to eight feet. She arched an eyebrow. "Really?" she said.

"Uh, I mean earlier," stammered Jay, exchanging a panicked glance with Frankie.

"I see," she said, like she didn't see at all and knew shibai when she heard it.

"Can we go now?" whined Punkin. "I want to get home in time to call Patrick before he goes to work."

"Hush," said Mrs. Machado. "Cool your jets."

Jay cleared his throat. "Anyway, I was just coming to thank you guys for the invitation, but I just remembered I told my Dad I would help him rake and bag the leaves."

More shibai. Jay and I raked and bagged them this

morning. I looked at my brother and swallowed the lump in my throat.

"Another time then," said Mrs. Machado. "Frankie! Quit standing around. Get in already." Frankie hustled to the side of the pickup and jumped in.

"Watch your feet, babooze!" griped Punkin. "Don't drip all over my bag! Watch your board!"

"Thanks again, Mrs. Machado. Laters, Frankie," Jay said.

"Laters, Jay."

They left.

Char Siu bumped me hard, knocking the umbrella almost out of my hands. "What's the matter with you?" she bawled. "I can't do this myself!"

I whipped around and saw she was trying to reel in the kite, but the twin lines were uneven and starting to cross. The clouds along the mountains were darker and a silvery mist had started to drift down the cliff sides.

"I said the rain's coming, lolo! You deaf?" she yelled over the wind. Char Siu was struggling to keep her footing and hang onto Iolani.

When had the wind picked up? This feels like a hurricane!

I took my umbrella and put the handle between my knees, ignoring the wind digging the umbrella's wires into my back and thighs. I reached out to Char Siu and took one of the lines. "Ready?" I shouted. "One, two, three, go!" We both started reeling as fast as we could. Iolani bucked and dove, cutting right, cutting left, before dropping into a death spiral. "Pull up!" I screamed. "Up!" A split second before impact, Iolani's wings caught the wind again and the kite rocketed skyward.

Jay was there, breathless from running. "Go!" he said, snatching the line from me. "Run! I've got this. If you hurry you might make it."

Without hesitating, I whipped the umbrella over my head and ran, the rain hiss, hiss, hissing at my heels all the way home.

9
ON THE ROCKS

~'Aumakua: a deified ancestor who takes on a specific physical form, such as a
shark, bird, octopus, eel, wind, dog, caterpillar, rock, shell, cloud, or plant.~

I was asleep; I knew it, just like I knew I was standing at
Piko Point on the lava outcrop that divided Keikikai and
Nalupuki beaches. Disoriented, I looked toward the pavilion
on the hill and for a second I saw two images—one from the
ocean looking to the shore and the other from the hillside
where Char Siu and I flew my kite.

I'm here, I thought.

The view from the pavilion disappeared. I took a breath
and tasted salt. Except for the time Uncle Kahana found
me, I'd never been to Piko Point; it was too dangerous for
me to be surrounded by all that water.

Behind me a voice chuckled, soft and low. I spun around
to discover a woman sitting on the cold, hard lava and gaz-
ing into the big saltwater pool.

She's beautiful.

"Uh . . . hello?" I said.

She didn't move, but spoke. "I'm sorry you're still half

buried in the ravine, Pohaku." Pause. "What? They did what?! That's so disrespectful to an 'aumakua stone!"

She paused again and smiled. "You're right. It could be worse, Pohaku. You could be stuck in some dusty museum and then I'd never have the chance to talk with you."

It's like she's on the phone.

I stepped closer and waved my hand in front of her face. "Aunty?" I said. " Ma'am?"

Nothing.

I'm invisible!

"A whole family of mongoose?" She shuddered. "Nasty foreigners, all of them."

I walked over to the water's edge and looked down. The moon wasn't quite full yet, maybe in another night or two, but it still lit the night sky like a lighthouse beacon. The ocean was calm, the sky was clear, and I could see the stars and moon reflected in the large saltwater pool near the woman's feet.

"Ah, Pohaku," she said. "All tourists are crazy. But when I woke this afternoon on the beach and found this man just staring at me, I didn't know what to do. He was so ashen I could feel the terror rolling off him in waves as kneeled down in the sand next to me. When he blurted he'd thought I was dead, I wanted to laugh. Later, when he asked if he could sketch me lying in the sand, I did laugh, but he was so earnest I let him."

She looked at the moon and shook her head, hiding her face in her long, dark hair. "You're right, of course. I should never have been napping on Keikikai beach in the sun. I need to forget about meeting Justin Halpert from California tomorrow morning, no matter what I promised. It's not worth it."

The woman sat there, hugging her knees and looking out to sea. As I watched, my belly began to cramp and my heart started beating faster and faster. I was afraid, but I didn't know why until out of the night he appeared, limping a little because of his missing right toe.

"Pua," he said.

"Kalei." She didn't turn around.

Kalei! The scary man with too many teeth is called Kalei.

"Talking to Pohaku, again?"

Pua nodded.

"Still forgotten in the ravine?"

"You could help me. We could dig him out," she said.

"Whatever for? Pohaku's useless."

"He wasn't once."

"The world has turned. He should sleep."

"'Aumakua guardians don't sleep," Pua said.

"Then let him rest his eyes," Kalei said.

Pua clicked her tongue.

"You weren't at the harbor this afternoon," he said.

"I'm sorry."

"I waited."

"I lost track of time."

"That's impossible."

She shrugged. "It's the truth."

Kalei stepped beside her and sat down. I breathed easier

when I realized he couldn't see me either. He reached out and fingered the edge of her kikepa, a long length of cloth wrapped around her like a sarong. "This is new," he said.

"Not really."

"I've never seen you wear it before."

She shrugged again. "I've had it for a while," she said, staring out to sea.

Kalei followed her gaze and sighed. "What's wrong?"

"Nothing."

"I don't believe you."

"It's nothing."

"Your lips are pale. When did you last eat?"

She shrugged.

"Pua," he asked, eyes narrowed, "did you come here this afternoon?"

Staring out to sea, she nodded.

He sucked his breath through his teeth. "On the sand? Were you on the sand at Keikikai beach this afternoon?"

She nodded again.

Kalei jumped up. "I knew it!"

She rested her forehead on her knees and closed her eyes.

Kalei balled his hands into tight fists. More afraid for the woman than myself, I stumbled over to her and wrapped my arms around her to shield her from Kalei, but my arms passed through her like smoke.

I'm a ghost, I thought, shocked. *There's nothing I can do.*

"He could kill you for this," he said.

Kill her? Who are these people?

Head on her knees, Pua nodded. "It might be easiest," she mumbled.

"Pua!" He threw his hands in the air. "What am I going to do with you?"

She shrugged and shook her head. He sat back down.

"Last time he beat you black and blue. He said if you did it again, he would kill you."

"I remember."

"Did you think he was joking?"

"No."

"What I am supposed to do? Telling Father would get us both in trouble, Pua. Is that what you want?"

"No."

"Do you want to die, is that it?"

She looked up. "No," she said, her breath emptying her lungs in a rush.

"Tell me why," he said. "Can you at least do that?"

She thought for a moment, as if she were choosing the right words to make Kalei understand. "One minute I'm fine, going along, doing the things I'm supposed to, and then I get an itch." She wiggled. "Right here, between my shoulder blades. I can't reach it. It drives me crazy, and I know the only thing that will stop it is going to the beach. This beach."

"There are other places to lie in the sun."

"I've tried. Do you think I want this? I know the risks."

"Do you?"

She glared up at him. I flinched and the look wasn't even for me.

"Pua, do you really understand what's at stake here?"

"Kalei, no matter what you think, I am not a child anymore. You can't scare me with the boogie man or giant squid or a hundred other things that go bump in the night."

"You should be scared," said Kalei. "I am."

"You are?" Startled, she forgot to be angry. "Of what?"

Kalei turned, faced the deepest part of the ocean, and spoke slowly. "Life is good now, Pua. There are fish in the sea. We have our 'aina and our home. We can travel wherever we want; people don't bother us. Life wasn't always this easy."

"Lying on Keikikai beach in the afternoon isn't going to change any of that. Like you said, we can go wherever we want. No one cares."

"Anywhere except here! What about Aunty Hanalei? She went to this beach and look what happened."

"That was a long time ago."

"People don't change, Pua. This beach is dangerous."

"I feel safe here," she said.

Kalei reached down and scooped water from the big saltwater pool where he stood. It slid like silver mercury through his fingers as he drizzled it over her feet. Pua wiggled her toes, flicking the drops away. Some of the drops passed through me, each one tumbling in the moonlight before landing in the darkness. I shuddered in relief.

"Your skin looks dry."

"Thank you for the compliments, brother dear. First, my lips are too pale, now my skin looks dry. Do I need to brush my teeth, too?" She bared her teeth at him and pushed his dripping hand away with her foot. "Knock it off."

He sat back down beside her on the barren lava, the starlight shimmering like water on the surface. "Just trying to help."

"Don't. You're just irritating me."

"Pua?"

"What?"

"You do have to brush your teeth."

"Oh!" She pushed him with her shoulder, happy he was no longer so angry.

He nudged her back. "Well, someone had to tell you."

She thought for a moment. "You're wrong about the 'aina," she said.

"We have our land," said Kalei.

"Not all of it," said Pua.

"What's done is done," Kalei said. "What do you want me to do? Run around waving signs, chanting 'Keep Hawaiian lands in Hawaiian hands'? That won't give us this beach back. Nothing will. Too many people think they own parts of it now."

"I know. It makes me sad."

"Makes me mad." He flicked a hermit crab back into the water.

"Kalei, I do know how dangerous it is for me to be here. If I could stop coming, I would."

"You're saying the 'aina is calling you? Is that it?"

She shrugged. "The itching doesn't make sense. You ever heard of anyone having an itch like that?"

"Yeah." He grinned. "Aunty Hanalei!"

She shoved him again. "Shut up and go if you're just going to make fun of me."

"You're the one talking chicken skin stories." In a high falsetto he mocked, "Kalei, the ʻaina, the ʻaina is calling me; I have to go to the mysterious itching beach or die!"

"Technically, the beach is scratching. I'm itching."

"Whatever, Pua," said Kalei.

Together they watched the ocean spray dance above the black lava as the waves crashed along the breakwater. The rhythm was soothing, like a heartbeat or drum. After a while, they leaned their heads together, both lost in thought.

I squatted down next to them and studied him, the man who caused me so much fear and panic over the years as I traveled with Dream Girl.

Why is this dream so different? I wondered. *Tonight Kalei's not a monster with too many teeth, he's a guy looking out for his sister. Why is Dream Girl so afraid of him? Is it her fear that makes me afraid?*

Sudden chicken skin blossomed on my arms and the hair rose on the back of my neck as I heard another voice speak in my mind.

(*Do not be fooled,*) it said. (*Your heart knows the truth.*)

I jumped. *Holy cow, what was that?!*

"I have to go away for a while," said Kalei. He lifted his chin to the ocean. "The ahi are running. Uncle Nalu says he needs my help."

"Do you want me to come?"

He shook his head. "No. One look at you and Uncle Nalu would know you'd been at the beach."

She touched her face. "I burned?"

"You glow." He grinned. "But seriously, I want you to stay away from Keikikai beach." He paused. "I can't make you."

"No, you can't."

"But will you? Please? For me?"

Pua contemplated the moon, but didn't answer.

Kalei sighed and looked to the sky. "Almost a full moon."

"Yes."

"Father left about an hour ago for the Big Island. When he asks, I'll tell him you went to Moloka'i for a while."

"To see Kamea. She's due soon. He won't think twice about that."

"At least that will help explain the tan. I hear all she wants to do is lie on the beach. I think she's trying to cook that keiki faster!" He stood. "Scratch that beach itch if you must, Pua, but be careful. You cannot afford to be seen, especially around here in the daytime."

He walked along the far edge of the saltwater pool to where it met deeper, swifter currents through a passage in the lava to the open ocean. He stretched his arms over his head, looking back at her one last time.

"Sun bathing causes cancer, you know. Night is the best beach time," he said, the moonlight glinting off his teeth, stark white against the shadow of his face.

Pua rolled her eyes. "Since when have you ever worried

about cancer? Enjoy your swim, Kalei. Tell Uncle Nalu aloha for me."

His face now grim, he called, "Remember Aunty Hanalei." He twisted backward, throwing his body into the darkness, and entered the water without a splash, diving down, down, down to the tunnel and open ocean.

"Show-off," Pua muttered. She stood, wrapping the kikepa tighter. "Sorry, about the interruption, Pohaku, but you know Kalei. It's all about him." She held out her hands in the moonlight. "But he was right. I need to eat. I also need to bathe. Oh, Pohaku, if you could see how chapped my skin is, rough from the sun, wind, and salt, you'd cry." She sighed, brushing sand off her feet. "I might as well go home, the worst is over." She fingered the edge of her kikepa. "A change of clothes would be nice. One of the catamaran sundresses, you think?" She turned towards the shore and clicked her tongue. "It's five hours to sunrise; there's plenty of time. I just hope Justin's an early riser. I can't afford to be in the sun too long."

"Zader! Zader, wake up," called Jay far, far away.

I woke with a snap. The blood from the gash made by my too-tight grip on my shark tooth necklace welled, dripping from my fist to stain the sheets. The pain in my palm chased away my last dream image of Pua stretching her arms over her head at Piko Point, reaching out to the moon like Kalei.

10
Scavenger Hunt

~Sprunch: a combination of Hawaiian Fruit Punch and Sprite mixed to taste. Highly addictive.~

"Wait, wait, wait!" Mom said. "Don't come in!"

"Okay," said Uncle Kahana at the front door. Ilima stood next to him, wagging her tail. "Kinda hard though to hand you these papaya through the screen."

Mom came to the door, hair in a messy bun, no makeup, and dark circles under her eyes. "Tell me you had the chicken pox already," she said.

"Yeah. Small kid time. Why?"

"Hallelujah! You can come in, but wash your hands before you go. Lili went to the doctor for her annual school physical for Ridgemont and brought home chicken pox! Paul, Lili, and Jay are all scratching away, driving me crazy."

"Ilima, you better stay outside," Uncle Kahana said. Ilima moseyed over to the side of the lanai, slumped down under a chair, and rested her head on her paws. She closed her eyes. "Good girl." She thumped her tail once.

"Liz, you're not sick?" asked Uncle Kahana.

"No. And neither is Zader."

"Zader never gets sick," Jay moaned from the couch. "Not even the sniffles. It's not fair."

Uncle Kahana opened the screen door and stuck his head in the room. "Howzit, Jay. I think it probably has something to do with his allergies. Aunty Lei never got sick either. She was always taking care of everybody else."

"I'd rather have chicken pox for a week than Zader's allergies!" Mom said. "Don't act like he's got it so easy just because this time he didn't get itchy red spots and you did!"

"Mom, I have them *inside* my mouth!" Jay pushed his head deeper into his pillow, hand on his forehead. "Hurts, you know!"

"Keep sucking ice."

Jay held up his empty glass. Mom rolled her eyes and walked to the couch.

Uncle Kahana flipped off his slippahs, entered the house, and walked to the kitchen.

"Howzit, Uncle," I said.

"Eh, Z-boy, howzit?" He set the papayas on the counter and picked up my sketchbook from the kitchen table, idly thumbing through it. Page after page of surfers on big waves, kids playing in the shallows on boogie boards, sunsets, canoe paddlers—there was even one of Uncle Kahana coming back from spearfishing. "Wow, Zader, you see everything." When he got to the end, he turned the book over and began flipping through it again. A sketch somewhere in the middle caught his eye. Partially colored, it was the one of Dream Girl in the floating red cloak. Uncle Kahana studied it for a moment, eyes too wide and mouth slightly open before turning the book toward me. "Who's this?" he asked.

I shrugged. "Nobody," I said.

He jiggled the book. "Get choke drawings of Nobody, then." He turned it back toward him. "You have a secret crush, Z-boy?"

I squirmed. "No."

"That's Dream Girl," Jay interrupted from the couch. "Zader sketches her all the time."

"Dream Girl?"

"He has nightmares about her."

"Shut up, Jay," I said. Uncle Kahana was looking at me funny kine. I reached for the sketchbook before he could say another word, but he twisted away from me, still studying the drawing.

Mom walked into the kitchen carrying an empty glass. She nodded at the book. "Good, yeah? I can't wait for Zader to take art classes at Ridgemont next year."

"Gotta get in first," said Uncle Kahana, still absorbed in the drawing.

Mom paused. "You don't think he will?"

Uncle Kahana looked up and shrugged. "I dunno, Liz. Plenny kids apply. Only a few get accepted to Ridgemont. Ridgemont's tough."

"His grades are okay," Mom said. She put the glass in the dishwasher and started loading the stack of plates by the sink.

"Okay only okay."

"Eh, who died and made you Zen Master? 'Okay only okay.' Sheesh. Grades are not the only thing they look at, you know. We'll figure something out. Get plenny time."

"Yeah." Uncle Kahana turned to me, finally handing the sketchbook back. "So, Zader, you're not sick?"

"No."

"Bored?"

"Little bit."

"Good. Liz, I'm taking Zader for the afternoon, maybe evening. Go get your waterproof jacket, the one with the hood."

"And umbrella," Mom said.

"Aw, Mom. It's not even cloudy!"

"Umbrella," Mom said.

"And bring your sketchbook stuffs too," said Uncle Kahana.

"And wash your hands, both of you. Zader, use the hand-sanitizer on the counter. I don't want you guys spreading more germs around town!" Mom said.

In less than a minute, Uncle Kahana, Ilima, and I escaped the house. I took a deep breath.

Freedom.

I checked the sky. "See? No clouds! Like I said, it's not going to rain!" I smacked the hibiscus hedge with my umbrella.

"Eh, don't take it out on the plants, Z-boy. Not their fault your mother loves you."

Abashed, I rolled my jacket around the folded umbrella

and tucked them under my arm. "I know she only makes me 'cause she loves me. It's a royal pain, though. Kids tease me all the time."

"How?"

"They call me Mary Poppins."

"Mary Poppins! Ho, that's funny!"

"Uncle!"

"Well, it is." Uncle Kahana gave me side-eye. "Does it matter more what people think about how you look or what you can do?"

"Huh?"

"If you didn't have an umbrella, then you probably couldn't be outside as much, yeah?"

"Yeah. I guess it matters more what I can do."

"Good, 'cause I have a surprise for you, but first we gotta pick up some things. First stop Aunty Mitsy's house."

Aunty Mitsy lived in a tiny four-room, box-shaped house with two big plumeria trees in the front and gardenia hedges along the walkway. Hanging from coffee cans suspended along the chain link fence were her pride and joy—sixty or so orchid plants—all different shapes and colors. Underneath the orchids were rows of miniature roses. Knocking on her front door was like standing in the perfume department at Macy's.

Uncle Kahana breathed deeply. "Smell that?"

"How can I not?" I said, wrinkling my nose.

"Wasted on you. Too young. Bumbai you're going like stuffs that smell li'dat."

Aunty Mitsy came around the side of the house,

watering hose in her hand. "Ah! I thought I heard some-body out here! Ai-yah! Zader! Try wait! I'm going to turn this water off!" Aunty Mitsy hurriedly turned off the hose. "Eh, Kahana, long time no see! You guys want to come inside for some guava juice? Get lemonade, if you like." Mitsy was already halfway through the front door.

Guava juice sounds good, I thought.

"Thanks, yeah, Mitsy, but Zader and I are kinda in a hurry."

Bummers.

"Oh?"

"I was wondering if we could borrow George's hip wad-ers, the old ones from his pineapple days."

"Those hammajang things? You can have 'em! They're just cluttering up the garage. You know George; he never likes to throw anything away."

"You sure? We could just borrow 'em. No need give 'em to us."

"Take 'em, take 'em. Twenty years, he's never used 'em. If he needs 'em, I'll tell him where they are."

She handed the dusty hip waders to Uncle Kahana who promptly handed them to me.

Of course I'll carry them, Uncle Kahana. Thanks for asking.

"Ah, Misty, these are perfect!"

"What're you going do with those old things?"

Uncle Kahana rested a finger alongside his nose. "A surprise, yeah? I don't want to spoil it."

Mitsy laughed. "Oh, Kahana, you're still kolohe!"

"Of course."

I brushed at the cobwebs and dust, trying to figure out why Uncle Kahana would need them.

They're old, but still solid, no deep cracks or rips. But please, let there be no centipedes crawling around inside. If I see one of those freaky things come roiling out the top, I'll scream like a little girl.

I held them out a little farther from my body.

"Thank your Aunty, Zader." Uncle Kahana said.

"Thank you, Aunty Mitsy," I said.

"You're welcome, welcome." Aunty Mitsy flapped her hands at us. "Now go away! Take your pilikia out of here! I gotta water my plants!"

Still grinning, Uncle Kahana led the way out into the street.

"Now what?"

"Next stop, Hari's."

Following Uncle Kahana around the store, I couldn't decide if we came for duct tape, peanut brittle, laundry soap, or—

"Ah. Here they are," said Uncle Kahana.

Yellow dish-washing gloves?

"Fo'real, Uncle Kahana? Why do we need those?"

"Patience, bullfrog, patience," Uncle Kahana said. "Bumbai you'll find out. Eh, Hari!"

"Eh, Kahana! How you doing?" Hari hustled out from the storage room, cigarette cupped in his hand and held behind his back.

"Fine, fine. And you?"

"Maikaʻi, mahalo." Hari coughed. "Just fine! What do you need today?"

"Just a package of gloves." He held them up. "Oh. And two large sprunches." Uncle Kahana glanced at me. "And one, no, two packages of chocolate cookies." Ilima pressed her wet nose against Uncle Kahana's bare leg. "Aieee! Eh, Ilima, you know I hate it when you do that! And two doggy biscuits for Ilima."

"No problem. Help yourself," Hari said. "I gotta get back to something I got going on in the back."

"Sure, sure," waved Uncle Kahana. "Zader and I can handle it. Zader, go make the sprunch, yeah? I'll bag the cookies."

Walking out of the store, I wondered not for the first time what the relationship was between Uncle Kahana and Hari. Uncle Kahana never paid for anything.

Weird.

"Now where?" I asked.

"My house. Actually, the storage area under the stairs."

At the storage door, Uncle Kahana looked around, then reached under the mat for the key.

"Wow, sneaky, ah, you," I said. "Where do you keep the house key, under a flower pot?"

"No. On the top of the door frame. Why? You wanna bust in?"

"Not me, Uncle. You're not scared somebody's going steal your stuff?"

"Psshtt. Who? What stuffs?" He tapped his head. "The most important stuff nobody can steal." He pushed open the door and turned on the light. "Okay, Zader. Go find my welder's mask. Should be on the left side in the back. I gotta go to do something else now."

"What?"

"Never mind your beeswax. Just go get the mask. I'll be right back."

Uncle Kahana waited until I entered the storage room before slipping around the door to the back of the building. I grabbed the helmet and followed.

He's hiding something.

Near the edge of the parking lot in a tiny wooden bowl half hidden under a taro plant, Uncle Kahana poured some of his sprunch. He opened a package of cookies and set them on the small lauhala mat next to the bowl. Putting the lid back on his drink, Uncle Kahana didn't see me peeking around the corner. I paused, then quietly stepped back and loudly shut the storage room door.

"I got it, Uncle Kahana," I called.

"Good, good," said Uncle Kahana as he hurried back. "Now we're going to the beach."

"Beach?"

"Beach."

STANDING ON THE SAND ON the Keikikai side of the lava divider, Uncle Kahana checked out his handiwork. "Not bad," he said. "Not bad at all." He circled me slowly, eyeing me up and down. The waders came to my hips. My coat came down to the tops of my thighs and over my arms. The tinted glass of the welder's mask covered my whole face and fitted over the hood of my coat. The dishwashing gloves covered my hands and fit under my sleeves. "Perfect," he said, rubbing his hands together. "School is now in session."

11
SCHOOLED

~'A'ole pilikia: no trouble at all.~

I held my arms away from my body, feeling like the little kid in that Christmas movie who couldn't put his arms down. "Uncle Kahana, I look ridiculous."

"At least you don't look like Mary Poppins anymore."

"No. Now I look like some weirdo from outer space."

Uncle Kahana tilted his head. "Nah, more like the janitor in a bio-tech lab." He reached out and adjusted my helmet. "Hot?"

"Little bit. Not too bad."

"Want more sprunch?"

"Yeah." Uncle Kahana slipped my straw under the glass visor for me. Sweet coldness hit the back of my throat cooling me from the inside out.

"Pau?"

"Yeah. Thanks," I said.

"Okay. Grab your sketchbook and pencil; we're leaving the rest of it here and going out there." He pointed to the lava divider between Keikikai and Nalupuki beaches.

"You're crazy. I can't go out there!"

Uncle Kahana laughed. "Try," he said.

I stood at the ocean's edge looking at the short walk through the water to the first of the lava rocks. "Tide's heading out," said Uncle Kahana. "Good time to see lots of critters." He motioned to Ilima. "Come," he said. He strode out onto the lava rocks without looking back. Ilima looked up at me, tongue hanging out and grinning her doggy grin. She jerked her head toward the ocean, then followed Uncle Kahana.

The first thing I noticed was the cold. The saltwater swirled around my knees, chilling my legs. It felt wonderful, better than an air conditioned movie, better than the sheets when you first get in bed, almost as good as shave ice. I wiggled my toes in the boots, pretending to feel the wet sand under my feet. "Uncle Kahana! It works!"

"Of course. What did you think, I wanted to kill you? Of course it works. Now come here. There's tons of stuff for you to see."

I climbed over the rocks, my hands baseball mitt clumsy as I used them to keep my balance. For the first time in my life I was outside at the beach without worrying about hidden puddles or random splashes. I felt giddy, like I'd spun around and around in circles on a swing. The sunlight was bright, too sharp near the water; flashes of light flickered like lighting along the bottom of the mask, making it all seem unreal. I reached Ilima first. She greeted me, wagging her tail in delight. Uncle Kahana squatted by a tide pool. "Come look," he said.

It took a moment for my eyes and brain to understand

what they were seeing: shadows of reds, blues, yellows, blacks, greens, and silvers darting into, under, and through cracks and ledges, skittering along the bottom, all shimmering in the clear water.

If I listen hard enough, I thought, *I'll hear them sing.* Startled, I shook my head. *If I get heatstroke, will Jay feel better?* I shook my head again. *Crazy thoughts, get out!*

"See the little one near the crack? The longish one with orange-red spots?"

"Yeah."

"That's pao'o. Haoles call them blennies. So's that green-spotted one. Get all kine blennies in here." Uncle Kahana moved along the edge of the pool, pointing to where the water was deeper. "Now those, the greenish-gray ones with the yellow spot and black stripes, you see 'em?"

"The ones by the black pokey stuffs?"

"By the wana, yeah. That's baby mamo, also called sergeant fish. When grown they're more silver."

Uncle Kahana leaned forward, resting his elbows on his knees. "This is wana." He pointed to a sea urchin with black spikes. "This is the bugger you have to watch out for. It lurks in the splash zone, hiding in cracks, waiting for a bare foot or 'okole."

"It attacks?"

"No. But it has a bad habit of living right where you walk, sit, or grab. The spines are venomous."

"Poisonous?" I asked.

"Poisonous is if you bite it and it makes you sick.

Venomous is when it bites you and you get sick. Wana are venomous."

I nodded.

"Zader, if you get a wana spine stuck in your foot, just pull it out, and tell your mom. She'll take you to the doctor and get medicine that will make it all better."

"Medicine? Is that what you used to do?"

Uncle Kahana laughed. "Me? No way. Small kid time, my uncles just pulled out the spines, slapped me on the back of my head for being so stupid, and 5-4-4'd on 'em."

"Go-shi-shi? On your foot?!"

"Of course! Back then people thought it was a waste of time and money to see a doctor for a wana sting. You had to lose the whole foot to see a doctor!"

As Uncle Kahana talked story, I watched bright butterfly fish play chasemaster and schools of yellow tangs—their elegant white spots as sharp as a surgeon's scalpel—cruising along a shelf. A spotted boxfish made me laugh; her expression was so somber, like at any moment now her mother was going to give her scoldings if she even thought about playing with the blennies.

"Now Zader, most of these fish are manini, real small kine, yeah? They're just babies. Their bigger ohana is outside the reef."

"How come I've never seen a bigger fish that looks like that?" I pointed to a blue and yellow one.

"Smart, ah, you? That's because some fish look way different when they grow up. For a long time scientists didn't know those two were the same fish. Sometimes girl fish can even become boy fish."

"Trippy."

"Fo'real. The ocean has plenny secrets. Only a fool thinks he knows them all."

We spent the couple of hours at the tide pools watching fish, anemones, starfish, sea cucumbers, snails, and hermit crabs. Uncle Kahana talked and talked while I sketched and labeled.

Through the gloves I held a sea cucumber, imagining its slimy texture oozing over my fingers. Uncle Kahana caught a brittle star before it could hide under a rock. On my hand its arms looked feathery and soft like a pipe cleaner, but all I could feel was the cool temperature of the water, slightly colder than my hands when I put it back.

"Enough lecture today, Zader. Your head's going to explode. Now I want you to check out different pools. Use your sketches to identify fish, anemones, things li'dat, and most important: watch, watch, watch! Observe what they eat. Who they chase. Where they hide. How they live. Bumbai I'm going to quiz you."

I smiled. "Shoots! Bring it!"

Uncle Kahana harrumphed. "Ilima, you keep an eye on Z-boy over here. I'm going talk story with an old friend over there." Uncle Kahana gestured to the Piko Point, the farthest point where the lava rock met deep ocean. "And don't try swimming! You're only kinda waterproof!"

With that Uncle Kahana turned and left me and Ilima by a tide pool halfway between Piko Point and the shore. We watched for a moment as his slippahs slap, slap, slapped the lava rocks, his old man's hammajang trunks hanging off his hips and hitched up again and again in time with his feet.

I stood and walked to the next large tide pool. After checking the area for wana, I decided to lie down on my stomach and peer over the edge. Ilima came and lay next to me, head on her paws. At first, I didn't see anything. Gradually, as the memory of my shadow faded, the residents came out of hiding and business began as usual. Hermit crabs carried their homes on their backs, picking through the sand for delicacies too small for me to see. Out of the corner of my eye, I saw a black line streak across the bottom.

"Ho, Ilima! You see that? I think that was an eel!" Ilima lifted a doggy eyebrow at me, looking like Spock. We watched until I spotted the eel again, moving like a snake along the bottom. Quicker than my eyes could follow, it snatched a fish and ate it in two huge gulps. "Whoa!" I said. Ilima closed both her eyes and settled in for a nap.

Look for things that don't belong. Those are the things that matter.

For some time nothing special happened. The blennies chased each other. Fish nibbled on limu and darted beneath rocks. After a while, my eyes kept returning to a peculiar rock tucked between two larger ones. No fish swam by it, and while it looked covered in limu, I didn't see the limu swaying in the water like it did on the rocks next to it. I leaned forward and looked closer.

My eyes blurred and stung for a moment, then my vision cleared as the rocks next to me swam into focus.

My whole body relaxed. I liked being nestled, my sides and back covered, leaving my eyes free to scan above and in front of me. I shivered a little, surrounded in cool, thick air—air like maple syrup, but easy to breathe.

When did the fog roll in? Good thing Uncle Kahana's miracle suit still works.

My fingertips tingled in the gloves and the taste of sweaty rubber filled my mouth. I heard an odd sound, a triple thump-da-thump-da-thump, and realized it was my hearts beating, two pulling air into my lungs and the third pumping blood through my body. With most of my legs curled beneath me, I reached out with one toe, tasting the air for information.

Ilima whined and nudged me with her nose. Startled, I blinked, my eyes sore from the glare off the water. I felt disoriented like I did when I had an allergy dream. I was itchy in the waders and my head ached. The inside of my mask was foggy from my breath. I tilted it away from my face and fanned some air inside. As I looked back into the water I saw the peculiar rock shift, then raise one tentacle, then two as it pushed off its ledge and glided across the bottom.

An octopus! Did it dream of me, too?

I pushed up on my hands and looked behind me. The sun was much lower in the sky, not quite setting, but close. I stood and when my legs stopped wobbling, I headed toward Piko Point and Uncle Kahana, Ilima leading the way.

He's asleep.

Uncle Kahana was sitting at the edge of a tide pool,

mumbling with his eyes closed and leaning against a stone that didn't belong on the reef. About the size of a basketball, it was gray and weathered, not black like lava.

That's Pohaku, I thought, then blinked. *How did it get here? Did Pua convince Kalei to dig him up? But that was just a dream, right?*

Maybe not.

As I got closer to Uncle Kahana I scanned the reef.

This saltwater pool at Piko Point's different. It's much deeper in the middle, maybe forty feet or more.

Instead of filling and draining through small fissures, channels, and tide changes, I could see a large archway leading to dark open water on the Nalupuki side. The ocean tide was coming in, and the water in the pool surged and ebbed with the waves. A fine mist floated in the air along the far side of the point as the incoming waves jumped the rocks and crawled down to the pool. Curious, I touched the water's surface. Through the gloves it was raw and cold, much colder than the other tide pools. It smelled of dark, deep things, things unseen and undreamed. I shuddered a little and withdrew my hand.

I walked over to Uncle Kahana and nudged his shoulder with my knee. "Uncle?" I said.

He cracked one eye. "Eh, Zader, where are your manners? Never interrupt your elders' conversation! Just wait a minute." He sighed and closed his eyes. "Sorry," he said. "Z-boy over there hasn't learned how to listen yet."

Elders? It's just me and him on the reef. Is he talking in his sleep?

"No, Pohaku, it's not Halloween. You know that's October! It's still August." With his eyes closed Uncle Kahana snorted. "Well, if you have a better idea for getting him out here I'd like to hear it!"

Nonplussed, I looked at Ilima, who I swear shrugged her shoulders. She came and sat at my side, nudging my hand with her nose and flicking it up on her head. "You want pets, Ilima?" I stood there, stroking Ilima's head and shoulders up and down, pausing once in a while to rub the area behind her jaws and ears.

Looking out over the reef I realized that the edge of Piko Point lined up with first breaks at Nalupuki.

Twenty feet! That's nothing! Standing at Piko Point, I can be out here with Jay and Frankie waiting for the next set! I looked down at my miracle gear and smiled. *I won't be stuck on the hill any longer.*

The sun was starting to set when Uncle Kahana at last opened his eyes.

"What you think of this place?"

"Uh . . . I dunno . . ."

"Dunno what? How do you feel being out here?"

"Uh . . . I like it?"

"You're not sure if you like it?"

"I do, I do. It's peaceful. I want to come back again."

He cocked his head at me. "Why?"

"Why?"

"Did the gear turn you into a parrot fish, Z-boy? You're repeating everything I say."

"Ah, no, no." I paused for a second, gathering my thoughts as I looked out at the ocean.

All that water! I should be terrified, but I'm not.

"I want to come back and watch Jay surf Nalupuki from here. I can see way better here than at the hill behind the pavilion. Plus, now I don't have to worry about getting splashed." I held out my arms and looked down at my feet.

Uncle Kahana grunted and eased his way up to standing. He patted the strange rock—*Pohaku, believe*—a voice echoed in my head—the rock that didn't belong.

"Aloha e Pohaku. I'll see you bumbai," Uncle Kahana said.

He turned back to me. "That's it? You want to come back to see Jay surf? You're not going to be embarrassed to be out here looking like that?" He gestured from my feet to my head.

I squared my shoulders, ashamed he had to ask. "No. You taught me it's more important to do what you want than to worry all the time about what everybody's thinking about you."

Uncle Kahana grunted again, giving me side-eye. He turned away from me and looked at the sunset.

The rhythm of the waves pounded in time to the pain in my head. All I wanted was dinner and bed, but I stumbled for the words, feeling like I'd somehow disappointed him. "This place feels good. I feel like I'm accepted here. The fish and crabs don't care what I look like or what I do. Everybody just does what they gotta. On this reef we just exist."

Without turning around, Uncle Kahana asked, "And what is this place? And if you say a reef or big lava rock, I'm going toss you over the side and you'll have to swim back."

I felt Ilima lean harder against my leg, steadying me. Like a slowly turning camera lens, the idea eased into focus. "It's a nursery," I said. "It's a place where young things grow in safety until they're ready for the open ocean." I held my breath.

It seemed like fo'days before Uncle Kahana turned around and faced me. He met my eyes and slowly nodded, "Very good," a smile breaking wide across his mouth. "Very, very good, Grasshopper. Maika'i!" He tipped his head to the side, his palms open and in front of his body. "But is this reef, this place, really *safe?*"

I thought back on all I'd seen today: bigger fish chasing littler fish; empty crab shells littering the black lava rocks; an eel on the prowl. "It's as safe as any place can be," I finally said. "Nothing's ever perfectly safe unless it's locked behind glass. If we want to live, we have to experience life outside the glass." I shrugged. "Wana, hermit crab, yellow tang—we all take chances in the end."

Uncle Kahana reached out and grabbed me around the shoulders, shaking me a little. "There's hope for you yet, Z-boy," he said. He wrapped his other arm around me and squeezed me tight. Ilima barked once, quick and sharp. Uncle Kahana released me. "All right, Ilima! Let's go." Uncle Kahana turned me around and gave me a little push toward shore.

Another brusque bark and Ilima slipped ahead, tail

straight in the air. "Eh, cool your jets, Ilima! The sun's not all the way down. No need to hurry, hurry, hurry all the time."

Ilima chuffed and daintily picked her way back to the beach, tail waving tall like a Japanese tour guide's flag.

Back on the grass, I took off the gloves, helmet, jacket, and waders and chucked them next to my art supplies. I wiggled my toes, happy to be free from my rubber skin. Uncle Kahana and I stood next to the showers at the pavilion and watched the sun end its day in a brilliant green flash.

"You know, some folks don't believe in the green flash," I said, sipping watery sprunch through my straw.

"That's because the stupid heads don't know how to look," Uncle Kahana said. "I've been watching the sun set in the ocean every night for more than seventy years. I've only seen the green flash maybe a couple hundred times. Some people look once, twice, maybe even for a whole week and never see it, so they think it cannot be. Foolish." He opened the chocolate cookies and absently put one in his mouth. Through the cookie he said, "Don't be a stupid head, Zader. Learn how to look."

I nodded and reached for the cookies. "Uncle Kahana, can ask you a question?"

"Shoot."

"How come you left cookies and sprunch under the taro plant by your house?"

Uncle Kahana looked skyward, searching for the first star. The sky was very clear and faintly pink, but night was coming on fast. "You saw that?"

I nodded, scanning for a star to wish on. Uncle Kahana rubbed the back of his neck, then rolled his head around his shoulders. He twisted his shoulders and hips until I heard his spine crack and reached his hands over his head and rocked a little from left to right, gently pulling on each wrist. Finally, he slowed, lowered his arms, and gave me side-eye. "I left it there for some very old friends. Maybe one day, after you learn how to look and listen, just maybe you can meet them." He looked at the pile of junk at our feet. "Take it. Everything. But you make sure you wear it all anytime you go near the water."

"Okay."

"I mean it. Anytime you're by the water, you wear it *all*. Promise."

"I promise." I tossed my empty sprunch cup into the rubbish can and gathered my magic suit—boots pointed this way and that, helmet dangling from the umbrella's handle above my shoulder, neon yellow gloves tucked inside, and my jacket's hood on my head. Before I headed home I met Uncle Kahana's eyes one more time. "Thanks, Uncle Kahana."

"No worries, Zader. 'A'ole pilikia for ohana, yeah? 'A'ole pilikia."

12
HERE'S TO YOU, MS. ROBINSON

~Ai ka pressah: the stressful feeling you get when you have five hours of work and two hours to do it; performance anxiety.~

"**C**'mon, Zader, we're going to be late!" Jay said, "and I don't want to be late the first day of school. Move it!"

I grabbed my backpack and umbrella and followed him out the door.

"Feels good, yeah? The last year we're going to Lauele Elementary, brah!" Jay said.

"Yeah," I said.

Good? NOT. Next year I'll be hoofing it alone to Lauele Intermediate, home of the longtime losers.

Jay gave me the once over. "How come you're wearing boroz? I thought the new clothes Mom and Lili bought you were sharp."

I shrugged. "Didn't feel like it."

I want my lucky shirt, not a new one with a tag that itches the back of my neck all day.

"What do you mean you didn't *feel* like it? Everybody wears their new clothes the first day of school! That's how you know who's boss!" Jay smoothed down his spotless t-shirt and ran his palm along the side of his head.

"They know already, Jay. We've been going to school with the same kids forever. Always the same."

"What's the matter, hah? You sick?"

I shook my head no.

"Smile already! It's another beautiful day in Hawaii nei. Lucky you live paradise, brah."

Must be nice to be Jay.

When he walked down the lanai to our sixth grade classroom, everybody gave him high-fives and shakas. Even guys he saw just yesterday at the beach acted like he'd been gone for months. Most guys gave me a small chin lift, their eyes sliding away, never quite meeting mine.

Whatever. If I surfed like Jay, they'd like me, too.

John Mayabuchi tried to throw his sports bag on a desk by Jay, but Jay was faster. "Zader! Quick! I saved the seat next to me for you!" he said.

I smiled for the first time this morning.

Who am I kidding? Everybody likes Jay 'cause he's Jay.

I sat down and checked out this year's classmates.

Frankie Machado. Char Siu! No way! We hadn't been in the same class since third grade. Becky Waters. Taylor Chung. Jerry Santos. Not bad.

Even though my lucky shirt was taggless, I felt an itch start on the back of my neck, a twitching between my shoulder blades. I turned around.

Alika Kanahele and Chad Watanabe. Crap.

"Devil," Alika mouthed, making his index fingers into

a cross. The bruising was still faint under his eyes and his nose was a little puffy.

I rubbed my nose and gave him stink eye.

He nudged Chad, then flipped me off. "Recess," he mouthed.

I rolled my eyes and turned around. By recess Alika would be in the principal's office or held inside copying lines from the dictionary. It was an empty threat.

Our teacher, Ms. Robinson, was new this year, and she was smokin'. Rumor had it she used to teach in Kailua, but moved to Lauele Elementary because she broke up with the school's principal. I also heard it was because she broke up with the school custodian, the school counselor, the band teacher, and best of all, one of her sixth grade students. Petite, with hapa-haole skin, blue eyes, and light brown hair, it was easy to believe any and all of the stories. She looked sweet and cute, the kind who had broken hearts strewn behind her like so many pieces of glass on the beach.

Cheerleader, I thought.

Until she spoke, that is.

"Class, come to order. My name is Ms. Robinson. My class is for learning. Those who want to talk, chew gum, goof around, speak only Pidgin, sleep in class, or come to school unprepared will be required to sweep the lanai, clean our class windows, pull weeds, and do other similar tasks for the remainder of the day. If you choose not to use your brains, you might as well spend your time developing your muscles. The world needs janitors, too."

I gulped.

Not cheerleader. Drill sergeant.

We all leaned back in our seats, all except Tunazilla who was busy picking her scabs.

"At the beginning of the week, you will receive assignments that are due at the beginning of the following week. If you work diligently, you will not have homework." The class cheered. Tunazilla yawned.

Maybe it won't be so bad.

Ms. Robinson raised her hands, quieting the class. "Unfortunately most, if not all of you, will not work diligently and will find yourselves becoming very familiar with various industrial strength cleaners." She paused, scanning the room, making eye contact with each of us. "However, if you choose to work hard in school, I promise to teach you as much as your head can hold. You'll never be bored. Once you've proven you can handle it, your school work will be individualized; in fact, you'll design most of your own assignments."

Lisa Ling's hand flew up. "You mean we can choose what we like study?"

Ms. Robinson smiled. "I mean that you can choose what you want to study. Want, not like. We speak English in my class, not Pidgin." She moved toward the whiteboard. "Take out a sheet of paper. We will begin with a math review." We scrambled to open our yellow peechee folders and pencil cases. She picked up a blue marker from its cradle and so casually—too casually—turned back to us.

"By the way, if any of you are interested in applying to private schools for seventh grade, you should know that for the last four years most of my students were accepted. In fact, three out of every five of my students who applied got into their first choices." She paused. "That includes Ridgemont."

Our jaws dropped. Ridgemont Preparatory Academy, grades seven through twelve, was funded by a perpetual trust worth billions. If you passed their tests and got in, the highest tuition rate was less than a tenth of what other private schools cost. Most kids paid little to nothing, donating a few hours a week to the cafeteria or library in exchange for a full-ride scholarship. Last year Lili and her friend Mele had to sweep the lanais after school, but this year Lili hoped she would be assigned a library job during her free period. Most of the library jobs were cushy—ten minutes of work, then the rest of the time to study.

Ridgemont graduates left for top tier colleges and came back as doctors, engineers, lawyers, teachers, and business owners. Most years only three, maybe four students in the whole Lauele Elementary School were accepted. Claiming three out of every five of your students got accepted to a school like that was like saying you'd walked on the moon.

Shibai, I thought, *shibai, shibai, shibai!*

I raised my hand. "Ms. Robinson, Ridgemont? How many of your students got in out of your whole class?"

Her smile reminded me of the Cheshire Cat. "Last year? Ten out of twenty-five."

Jay raised his hand. "Ten out of twenty-five isn't sixty percent. It's only forty percent. You said three out of five, which is sixty percent."

She arched an eyebrow and nodded. "Very good. What's your name?"

"Jay."

"Jay?" She looked at her roll.

"James Kapono Westin. I go by Jay."

"You're correct, Jay, ten out of twenty-five isn't sixty percent. However, I said sixty percent got into their first choice. Only ten students had Ridgemont as their first choice. One went to Punahou, one to Kamehameha, two to Iolani, and one to St. Louis. How many does that make?"

Jay thought for a moment. "Fifteen. Fifteen out of twenty-five is sixty percent."

Frankie Machado raised his hand. "You taught the gifted program, yeah?"

I didn't see how it was possible, but her grin got even wider. "Technically, no. However, I believe all my students are gifted. Let's continue the problem Jay started. How many of my students did not get into their first choice school? Show your answer as a fraction and percentage."

Maybe, just maybe with her as my teacher I might have a chance!

13
RUN-FU

~A'o i ke koa, e a'o no i ka holo: when you learn to be a warrior, you must also learn to run.~

"He knew we were coming, right?" Char Siu said.

"Yeah," I said. "Three o'clock."

"It's after three now," said Jay. "You think Uncle Kahana and Ilima forgot?"

"Nah, no way," I said. "He reminded me yesterday."

"Try knocking again," Char Siu said.

I raised my hand, but before it touched the door, it opened. "What?" scowled Uncle Kahana.

"Uh, howzit, Unclc," I said.

"Go away." He shut the door in my face.

We stood there just looking at each other. "What now?" Jay asked.

"Something's not right," Char Siu said.

"You think?" said Jay.

"Knock again, Zader."

"No way," I said.

"I'll do it." Jay tapped on the door. "Uncle?" he called, "Uncle Kahana! It's us. We're here for the lesson."

The door popped open. "What? You guys selling cookies, lau lau, or band candy?"

"Uh, no, Uncle. We're here for Lua," Jay said.

"You need a bathroom, go downstairs. Hari has a public lua in the back of the store. This is a private residence." This time he slammed the door.

"What's wrong with Uncle Kahana?" asked Char Siu. "Why is he mad at us?"

"Should we go?" I asked.

"You think he's lost it just like Frankie's grandpops? Old guys can just snap. Maybe we better get Hari," Jay said.

From behind the door we heard a muffled sound, like a cough or a wheeze. "Shhhhhh!" said the door.

Char Siu cocked her head. "Where's Ilima?" she asked.

On cue the door began to growl, low and deep. I looked at Jay's arm and saw the chicken skin rise, echoing the chills I was feeling tingle up and down my spine.

I glanced at Char Siu, but she was shave ice cool, watching the door. "We are stupid heads," she said, and scratched on the door with her nails, a politely soft sound. She leaned close to the door jam and whispered, "Pono."

The growling stopped as the door cracked open barely wide enough for Uncle Kahana's eye to peer out at us. He said not a word.

Char Siu bowed her head. "Aloha, Kumu. We are sorry we are late."

Uncle Kahana's eye looked out at us, saying nothing.

Char Siu looked up, then quickly back down. She jabbed me with her elbow. "C'mon!" she hissed.

Jay and I bowed our heads. "Sorry, Kumu," we said.

"Harrumph!" he snorted, blowing the air out in one giant rush. "What time is it?"

"Uh, three-ten, something like that," said Jay, still looking down.

"And what time I did I say, Zader?"

"Three o'clock."

"Harrumph!" he snorted again. "What else I did I say, hah?"

"Huna na mea huna," said Char Siu.

"And that means banging on my door, shouting to the world you like go 5-4-4?"

"No, Kumu," she said. "It means keep sacred things secret—the opposite of saying we're here for our Lua lesson."

"It means proper respect," I said. "We were thoughtless, Kumu. It won't happen again."

"Harrumph!" he snorted for a third time. "You have anything else to say to me?"

"Ae, Kumu," said Char Siu, raising her eyes to his. "Pono."

The eyeball moved to me. "Pono," I said.

"Pono," said Jay.

"Maikaʻi," said Uncle Kahana, throwing the door wide. "E komo mai. Leave your slippahs outside."

As we came through the door Ilima greeted us all with a lick, then retired to her pillow stashed under kitchen table again. Like before, the furniture was pushed out of the way, but this time a section of the floor was padded in lauhala mats and old cushions I recognized from the chaise lounges on the lanai. Jay grinned at the padding and swung his arms, ready to rumble. There was a smell—fresh and crisp and green in the air—that led me to a glass bowl resting on the kitchen counter.

"Maile lau liʻi and ʻolapa," said Uncle Kahana, breathing deeply. "Although we don't have an altar like a proper pa lua, it didn't seem right to begin without something to remind us of the traditions of our fathers—and mothers." He smiled at Char Siu. "Like life, everything about Lua is symbolic. Smell 'em?" We nodded. "The maile smells strong, yeah? It represents the body. A strong, healthy body has an odor—sweat—very distinct. We work, we play, we live, we sweat. Death also has a smell, a rotten, putrid pilau stink. Lua is about balance. In the pa lua the strong fragrance of maile reminds us of the balance between life and death."

"And the ʻolapa?" asked Jay. "It's not strong like maile."

"The ʻolapa branch represents throwing aside what troubles you, sweeping away those who would harm you or have evil intentions or thoughts toward you."

"Alika-dem," I said.

"Maybe," said Uncle Kahana. "It represents everybody who threatens you, known and unknown."

"Kumu, are we going learn some Lua throws today?" Jay asked tapping the mats with his foot.

"Bumbai. First we stretch."

He worked us slow and steady, loosening joints and lengthening muscles, stretching places between ankles and shoulders and knees and hips I didn't know I had. Jay didn't say a word, but I could feel him twitching, the energy humming through his body.

Jay's bored. He wants to fight.

"Okay, gang, pau for now. Make sure you're stretching every day. Your bodies need to become more flexible and strong before I can even begin to teach you the simplest lua 'ai I know."

"'Ai? What's lua 'ai?" asked Char Siu.

"'Ai means form or hold or throw—Lua techniques. Every technique has a name."

"How many 'ai are there?" asked Jay.

"Hundreds. Thousands," said Uncle Kahana.

"How many do you know?" Jay pressed.

"Enough."

"How many? Thousands? Hundreds?"

Uncle Kahana looked at Jay, an odd smile on his face. "Enough," he said again. "Each Lua master and school had their own set of 'ai. Next time—"

"Uncle Kahana, we are really done for the day?" Jay asked. "All we did was stretching and hopping around. I thought we were going learn to Lua."

"Not enough action for you, J-boy?"

Jay paused. He knew he was on dangerous ground, but didn't know where to place his foot. Finally he shrugged. "I want to learn more," he said.

"More?" Uncle Kahana asked. "Why?"

"Because I can do more. Besides, you never know when trouble's coming. If we don't prepare now, it's too late."

Uncle Kahana shifted his weight and tilted his head.

Finally he nodded. "You have a point, Jay. Okay, haumana, sit down. We'll begin with the first lua ʻai I ever learned." He motioned to the mats and waited until we were seated. He rubbed his hands together. "This ʻai is very simple, but powerful, the most important lua ʻai you will ever learn."

Jay leaned forward, holding his breath.

"It's called...Run-fu."

"Hah?" said Jay. "Run-fu?"

"That's not even Hawaiian," said Char Siu.

"You guys heard of Kung-fu?"

We nodded.

"Kung-fu is a Chinese style of fighting. This lua ʻai is smarter. Run-fu is what you do so you don't need Kung-fu."

"Run?" squeaked Jay.

"Exactly. Before you learn how to fight, you gotta learn how to run."

"That's the most important lua ʻai? Run? I thought Lua masters were fierce!" said Jay.

"Balance, Jay, balance. No shame in running if you're outnumbered, outmatched, and going to make die dead."

"What if they call you chicken?"

"So? Just because they call you chicken you're going to lay an egg?"

"No."

"Lua is about using your brain, not just your muscles. Always live to fight another day, Jay. Live to win another day."

"Kumu," said Char Siu, "what if you can't run?"

"Then you go for lua ʻai number two: Kill-fu." All joking

was gone. Uncle Kahana was gone. In his place stood an ʻolohe lua regarding us with his thousand year eyes. "To be pono, you don't strike first and you always try to find other ways. But if your back is against the wall—or the backs of those you love or must protect—don't hesitate, don't fool around. Kill-fu. Clear?"

"Ae, Kumu," we said.

"Maikaʻi," he said. "Now who wants some sprunch?"

14
ALIEN SPACE WALK

~Nah nah nah nah nah, brah: just kidding.~

"**Z**ader," Jay called, "This is the last wave. I'll meet you by the showers."

From my perch near Pohaku at Piko Point, I watched Jay paddle to the sweet spot and coast into shore. The sun was still high with a couple or more hours of daylight left, but we both had homework and it was a school night. Mom would be home soon, and while she knew we were at the beach, she didn't know Jay was surfing at Nalupuki. We wanted to keep it that way.

I adjusted the welder's helmet and scrunched my toes in the waders, getting ready for the long hike to the pavilion. I looked up to judge the distance and froze.

Coming across the lava, barefoot and in no hurry, was Kalei.

I looked around. No place to go, no place to hide.

Maybe if I head toward Keikikai, he won't see me.

I couldn't move, couldn't breathe. I didn't even wonder that he was here, on the reef, walking towards me. This

wasn't a figment of my imagination, the result of too much crabmeat or a rare chunk of steak.

Underneath my jacket, the shark tooth necklace warmed against my skin. I touched it through the layers of glove, jacket, and shirt and felt the hard outline, an irregular triangle near my heart.

Don't bleed. Don't grip so hard it cuts you.

And still Kalei kept coming, over the rocks and around the saltwater pools. I had to do something fast.

I tucked my umbrella under my arm and forced my legs to move. Mechanically, I placed each foot carefully in front of the other like an astronaut walking on the moon, each step bringing me closer to him, the man from my dreams with the too-sharp teeth.

When we were close enough to speak, he didn't pause. He glanced at me, barely a side-eye, curious, but beneath his notice. I held my breath, keeping my eyes down.

We passed.

I didn't look back until I reached the grass below the pavilion. Piko Point was empty; the entire lava flow was empty. I flipped off the helmet and scanned both Keikikai and Nalupuki beaches. Nothing.

"Look, Alika," said Chad. "An alien from outer space."

"That's not an alien, that's a devil," said Alika. "If I had some water, I'd show you."

I moved the helmet and umbrella to my left hand and glanced right and left. Nobody, no help, nowhere. "I don't want to fight, Alika."

"Too bad," he said. "We like beef with you." He moved closer, stepping in front of Chad.

"Why?"

He blinked. "Why?" He looked at me like I was crazy. "Because we can," he said.

I dropped everything and moved into the ready stance Uncle Kahana taught me, weight balanced, knees bent, back straight, and fists clenched near my thighs.

Chad laughed. "What is that? Alika, he looks like he's taking a—"

BAM! A flying surfboard soared through the air and cracked Alika on the back of the head.

"What, Alika? Never learn yet?" said Jay.

"That's 'cause he's one special kine stupid," I said.

Alika kneeled on the ground, hand on the back of his head. "Ah, Jay, you bugger, we were only joking!'

"Me, too," said Jay. He reached down and picked up his board. "Wanna joke some more?"

"Keep your freaky brother away," shouted Chad.

"Oh, you wanna joke around, too, Chad?"

"Nah nah nah nah nah, brah," said Chad. "Wasn't me."

"No, Chad doesn't like to joke," I said. "He likes his nose where it is."

Chad dropped his eyes, mumbling something I couldn't hear as he helped Alika to his feet.

"Yeah, Chad, pau games today. Better take Alika home. You know the drill," said Jay.

When they were gone, I picked up the helmet and umbrella and gestured to his board. "Ding it?" I asked.

Jay checked both sides, then shrugged. "Alika's got a hard head, but I think the board's okay. Let's go. Mom'll be home soon and I don't want her coming to find us." Completely ignoring Alika and Chad whispering in the parking lot, Jay turned towards home. Halfway there, he gave me side-eye.

"Run-fu?"

"Wall," I said. "Plus hard to run in waders."

"Truth," he said.

15
JAWS JUNIOR

~Chicken skin: spooky, scary feeling; goosebumps.~

I was sitting on a lump of lava rock at Piko Point running a piece of driftwood I'd found around and over my fingers. It was difficult to feel the fine, smooth grain through the gloves, but I kept getting glimpses of something hidden in the wood.

A dolphin? Maybe a whale, I thought. *No, this line is all wrong.*

Overhead, the sky darkened. Startled, I looked up, afraid a storm had blown in.

"Yeah, Z-boy, I see that look in your eye. What's the matter, hah? Just now you figured out it could rain?" said Uncle Kahana. Over his shoulder was my umbrella with my welder's helmet hanging from it like a hobo's tote. I'd left them at the pavilion next to my sketchbooks and pencils.

"Uncle Kahana." Ilima yipped and wagged her tail, coming in close, hoping to get a few pets. "Howzit, Ilima." I patted her with one hand and held the driftwood away with my other. "No, girl, the stick's not for you. It's mine."

Towering above me, Uncle Kahana glared, waves of

disappointment crashing down. "I'm glad to see you out here, Zader. Not so glad that you don't have your helmet or umbrella."

Crap. Here we go.

I sighed. "Just don't tell Mom, okay, Uncle? There's not a cloud in the sky, plus the ocean's so calm today, I'm not going get splashed if I'm careful."

Uncle Kahana grunted and dropped the umbrella and helmet at my feet. Ignoring me for the moment, he turned and placed his spear and goody bag full of fish at the edge of the saltwater pool. He placed both his palms flat against Pohaku's round sides, closed his eyes, and muttered something under his breath. He leaned down and touched his nose to the rock's surface, inhaling deeply.

Crazy. Uncle Kahana is nuttier than a Snicker's bar. Should I stay or go? I glanced at Ilima. *Wait! Did she just roll her eyes and shrug?* I looked closer. *Winked! She winked at me.*

"Ilima?"

She turned and bit her flank, nibbling on a fleabite.

Dog. She's a dog.

Ilima chuffed and grinned her doggy grin.

What if I'm the crazy one here?

Uncle Kahana muttered again, patted the rock, and opened his eyes. He squatted next to me, tapping the helmet with his finger. "It only takes one time, Zader."

"It's not like that, Uncle Kahana. Watch. I can pull my hood up and zip my waterproof windbreaker all the way—"

I stood up, zipped, and pulled the hood strings around

my face until only a small part of my nose and eyes were showing. "See? Almost no way I can get wet now!"

"Yeah, I see," said Uncle Kahana. "I also see that you can't see exactly where you're going when your coat's zipped up like that. It's easy to trip and fall into the ocean. I also see that even though you can wear your jacket that way, you weren't, Z-boy." He shook his head. "How come?"

I looked down at the driftwood in my hands, then up again at Uncle Kahana. "Hot," I mumbled.

"Bulai," said Uncle Kahana. "You're not sweating. I've never seen you sweat. It can be ninety degrees and you in long sleeves and long pants in the sun and you still never get hot and sweaty." He looked toward the beach pavilion near the showers. "I dunno. Maybe it was better when you stayed away from the water. Safer."

"But I like it out here."

Uncle Kahana tipped back his head, looking at the sky. He blinked a little in the bright light, then reached over to the big saltwater pool to wash the last traces of fish blood and scales from his hands.

"When Jay-dem had chicken pox and you were driving your mother crazy because you weren't sick, I thought there had to be a way to get you out here. What kind of life was it for you up there drawing and watching when everybody's down here having fun? How could I protect you, keep you safe from all that water and pain, but not alone by yourself? How could I teach you about living on an island when all you know is land?" Uncle Kahana touched the water again, tickling it with his fingers. "Then I thought of the waders and welding helmet. Perfect! I could cover you from head to toe and put dish gloves on your hands—no way a single drop would touch you. You can be out here even if it's only on the lava flow observing the tide pools and learning a little bit about the rest of this world."

I hung my head, feeling a little bit shame. I rolled the driftwood between my palms, thinking.

He gestured to the water all around us. "But here you are, no protection, easy protection, I think, between you and all this pain."

He flicked a saltwater drop off his fingertips. "Why?" he asked.

I shrugged. "I guess I just didn't want to wear it."

Uncle Kahana snorted. "Well, at least you're honest," he said. "But I promised your mother—"

I sensed it first, some motion out the corner of my eye, color darting too fast against the sun. I flipped off my jacket's hood and whipped my head toward the Nalupuki shoreline in time to see someone claw his way out of the ocean, surfboard under one arm, the other waving wildly. "Shark!" he screamed. "Shark, shark, shark!"

"Jay," I said, and then I was gone, running full-tilt over the rocks to the beach, Ilima at my heels.

"Confunit!" said Uncle Kahana rising more slowly and carefully working his way to the Nalupuki shore. With the shouts of "shark" traveling up and down the beaches, the line up at Piko Point was abandoned as all of the Nalupuki surfers headed in. Mothers along the Keikikai side were wrapping kids in towels and herding them to the pavilion showers.

Above the water line at Nalupuki, Jay stood in the middle of a loose group of surfers, his face white and his board gripped tight with bloodless fingers. "How big?" someone asked, but Jay just shook his head, eyes to the ocean. I stood next to him, my gloved hand on his bare shoulder and our bodies carefully apart so the saltwater dripped harmlessly down Jay's body. I ignored the crowd, my eyes scanning the water, up and down the beach and along the horizon. Around our legs Ilima was dance, dance, dancing, churning up the sand. My nose twitched and my skin itched, ripples like water running down my spine. I could feel Jay's energy thrumming through him; his heart pummeling against his ribs. Like me, his eyes were searching, watching, waiting, just like the feeling that comes from a nightmare in the middle of the night with the wind scratching at the window and the closet door creaking open.

"Kulikuli already, Ilima," said Uncle Kahana stepping off the lava flow and crossing the sand toward us. He flicked his wrist, telling her down. "No need to act like that. No blood. No bites. 'Nuff, already."

Ilima chuffed and sat at Uncle Kahana's feet, ears perked.

"See, Ilima? Nothing to worry about." Uncle Kahana stood there, letting his calm work its way through the crowd. He rolled his shoulders and cracked his neck, the ordinariness of him standing there in the sand helping the high-wire stress of the gathered surfers ease away. Color came back to Jay's face and everyone started remembering places they had to be.

"Ah, the waves are junk today. It's getting late." Frankie scratched his chest, rubbing away the salt. "Eh, Jay, I'll see you tomorrow," he said, picking up his board and heading for the showers.

"Shoots," said Jay, still looking at the waves. "Tomorrow's supposed to be better."

"Yeah. Laters," said Frankie with a head bob at me and Uncle Kahana.

"Howzit, Uncle Kahana," said a voice behind us. I turned and there was Nili-boy, hair ocean-wet and slicked off his face. "Little Cuzes." He bumped fists with Jay and raised howzit eyebrows at me. Ilima barked. "Oh, and of course, you, girl. I'm never going to forget you!" cooed Nili-boy as he dropped to the sand to ruffle her ears.

"You surfing today?" asked Uncle Kahana.

"Nah," said Nili-boy. "Too small. I was just catching rays waiting for Nalani to get off work."

"Nalani, that's Hari's new cashier, yeah? The real pretty wahine with the green eyes?" asked Uncle Kahana.

"Yeah," sighed Nili-boy.

"When did you start seeing each other?" Uncle Kahana wiggled his eyebrows.

"I've always seen her; she's never seen me." He laughed. "Yet."

Uncle Kahana grinned. "Wahine like that, ex-*pan*-sive!"

"Worth it."

"You working?"

"Surfing every day."

"Psshtt. That's not work," Uncle Kahana sniffed.

"Eh," said Nili-boy, "if people want to pay me to surf, I'm going to let them."

Through the glove I felt Jay's pulse continue to slow and his breathing ease; morning had come and the boogieman was no longer in the closet. I saw Nili-boy and Uncle Kahana exchange side-eye, a whole conversation I didn't hear.

"You're what, twenty-something now and still surfing every day?" said Uncle Kahana.

"When the waves are good enough to pay," Nili-boy said. "But braddah Jay over here, he's the real talent in the family." Nili-boy bumped Jay's thighs with his shoulder. "I saw him at the last Menehune Surf Meet at Sunset. He represents."

Jay didn't move or turn his head. He was still watching the waves and the water.

Uncle Kahana and Nili-boy exchanged another look.

"Jay," said Nili-boy softly, "What's the haps?"

"I saw . . . I think I saw a shark," said Jay.

"Who's a pretty girl, hah?" Nili-boy gave Ilima a final ear ruffle and stood with a shrug. "Probably. Get plenny sharks out there. Probably more than one." He bent down to brush the sand off his knees, making more side-eye conversation with Uncle Kahana. He nodded slightly at Uncle Kahana's raised eyebrow. Uncle Kahana rolled his eyes.

I'm missing something.

Jay bit his lip and nodded. "I think there were two. One was big." He looked at Nili-boy, taking his eyes off the water for the first time. "Really, really big."

"J-boy, you seen sharks out there before?" asked Uncle Kahana.

Jay wiped his hair off his forehead. "Sometimes."

"Big ones?"

"Mostly small kine. I've seen a few big ones. But this was . . . different."

"Different how?" asked Nili-boy. "Different color, different fins?"

Jay looked at the ground, pushing sand with his toes. "I dunno how. I got chicken skin, yeah? Then I saw 'em and I knew."

Uncle Kahana nodded. "And then the sharks attacked you?"

"What? No, they—"

"Bumped your board?" asked Nili-boy.

"No!"

"Circled you?" asked Uncle Kahana.

"No—it—they—they were headed toward the rocks," said Jay with a chin lift to the lava flow. "Toward Piko Point."

"Ah," said Uncle Kahana, eyeing the rocks. "They were headed to the point. So why panic?"

"Uncle Kahana," I said.

"No, no, no, I want to know why Jay came flying up the beach like Jaws was on his 'okole."

"The one I saw, the one I saw for sure was big. Really big."

Nili-boy saw the tears form in Jay's eyes and cuffed him in the arm before they could spill. "No worries, Jay. Akamai, yeah, to get out of the water when you don't feel safe. But you gotta do it slowly. No panic. Chill. Sharks can tell when there's panic. Makes 'em want to bite."

Uncle Kahana nodded. "Ocean's theirs; we're guests. Being a good guest means leaving when they want to use the beach, but slowly, with respect. Running away makes everybody forget their manners."

"Makes you look like a snack," laughed Nili-boy. "And while you might make it to the beach, but what about everybody else?"

It snapped into place like the puzzle piece you never thought would fit. "Prey runs," I said, looking directly at Nili-boy.

He flinched and I looked away. I heard him swallow, then clear his throat.

"Usually," said Nili-boy, "prey runs, but sometimes mistakes happen. That's why you always wear a ti leaf lei when you surf. You have one, right?" Nili-boy lifted his foot, showing his twisted ti leaf anklet.

"No," said Jay.

"What? What's the matter with you?" Nili-boy slapped Jay's shoulder. "Didn't Aunty Liz teach you that every time you go in the ocean you wear a ti leaf lei—ankle, wrist, neck, same-same, it doesn't matter where."

"No," said Jay.

"No?" Nili-boy's eyebrows were almost off his head.

"Liz's mom was more, ah, modern," said Uncle Kahana. "I should've told them."

"You have a lei, Uncle Kahana?" I asked.

He held out his wrist. A thin, dried out double strand ti leaf lei looped around it, salt cracked and water stained.

"Of course Uncle Kahana wears a lei when he gets in the water. He wants to make sure the sharks going to know who not to bite!" Nili-boy shook his head. "Come, Little Cuz, let Big Cuz show you how. There are ti plants growing by the showers. Go pick ti leaves. I'll meet you over there."

Jay looked at the plants, then at Nili-boy's ankle and Uncle Kahana's wrist. "Fo'real?" he asked.

"Go," said Uncle Kahana. "And you, Z-boy, go with Jay. You can hold his board while he picks."

KAHANA WATCHED THE BOYS WANDER to the ti plants near the showers, heads bent over the driftwood, a careful space between them. When they were far enough away, he turned back to Nili-boy.

"An'den?" Kahana asked.

Nili-boy shrugged, shading his eyes against the setting sun as he scanned the Nalupuki ocean, moving from shore to first breaks to horizon and back.

Kahana reached down to touch Ilima's head. "Real pilikia or too much TV?" he asked. "What do you think, girl?" Ilima closed her eyes as he scratched behind her ears, then reached up and licked his hand. She whined and did it again. Kahana paused, turning his hands over and over remembering. "I washed my hands in the big pool at Piko Point," he said. "They had fish blood and scales on them."

Nili-boy lifted his chin to Piko Point where a young woman and a girl stood looking back at the beach. The woman held up the bag of Kahana's fish, saluted, then jumped into the saltwater pool feet first. The girl stood a moment longer, watching the shore, then dove into the pool. "Looks like you don't have a dinner," said Nili-boy.

Kahana sighed.

On the way home Jay shifted his board and nodded at the driftwood in my hand. "An'den," he said.

I shrugged. "Maybe something for Lili for Christmas," I said, holding it up.

"Dolphin?" he said.

I shook my head. "Nah. I think the line's wrong. Some kind of fish, though." He took it from my gloved hand and turned it over and around.

"Whatever's in here, you'll find it," said Jay. "Just like the turtle you carved for Mom's birthday."

"You think she really liked it?"

"Of course! It was awesome. Better than the ones guys sell down by Waimanalo."

"Really? I thought the back fin was a little short."

"Nah. Even if you looked close, nobody could tell."

16
School Daze

~Kulia i ka nu'u: strive to reach the highest.~

M s. Robinson's sixth grade class was noisy the day we came back from Thanksgiving break. Nobody wanted to focus on fractions; everybody wanted to go outside and talk story about the holidays. Ms. Robinson took pity on us and let us out for recess a little early. Everyone except me.

"Zader? Can you come over here for a minute?" she asked.

Great. Her minutes last forever.

"Sure," I said, walking over to her desk. She reached into a drawer and pulled out a crumpled piece of paper, flattening it out on the desk.

Crap. Now I'm in trouble for wasting paper.

"I found this in the rubbish can after the class holiday party. Is it yours?" she asked.

"Yeah." I bit my lip.

Here comes the lecture.

She turned it a little so we could both see it. With the tip of her finger she lightly traced the outline of the shark I drew during language arts. "It's very good," she said.

I blinked.

She turned it completely toward me. "What can you tell me about it?"

I shrugged. "I was just doodling," I said. "It's nothing."

She turned the paper back toward herself. "It's not nothing!" she said. "It's sparse, just a simple line drawing. I agree with you there. But that's what makes it so powerful. What were you thinking when you drew it?"

I shook my head. "Nothing much. I was thinking about the driftwood I found and how the image inside wasn't a dolphin or a whale. As I was picturing the wood I drew this." I gestured at the paper.

"You're carving this out of wood?"

I nodded. "Yeah. For my sister Lili for Christmas. The wood caving's better than this drawing, though. I kinda ran out of time when language arts ended early, so I threw it away."

Oh crap! Did I really say that?

Ms. Robinson raised an eyebrow, but chose to ignore it. "Zader, do you have any other sketches?"

I walked to my cubbie and took a folder out of my backpack. "Here're some better drawings," I said as I handed her the folder. "At least I took more time with these."

Ms. Robinson sorted through the papers and spread some out on her desk. She didn't say anything for a long time, just stood there looking at them and occasionally shuffling a new one to the top. No one had ever looked at my drawings the way she did. I found myself bouncing from foot to foot like I was getting ready to run a race.

When she came to the sketches of Dream Girl, she paused, holding one out to me.

"Who's this?" she asked.

"Nobody. Just a girl."

"Hmmm," she said, giving me side-eye. She flipped it over and saw one I made of Kalei standing at Piko Point. She shuddered. "And this one?"

I shrugged.

"His eyes . . . so cold. Like he doesn't care about anyone or anything." She moved to the bottom. "Carving and sketching," she muttered, shaking her head. She looked at me. "Zader," she said, "all this is amazing. Where did you learn to draw? What's your favorite medium?"

Where did I learn to draw? How does anyone?

"I don't understand the question," I said. "I'm always drawing—backs of envelopes, grocery receipts, scratch paper, whatever."

Ms. Robinson looked at me with an odd expression I couldn't read.

"Jay surfs," I finally said. "I draw."

Ms. Robinson nodded, slowly. She slid the papers around, bringing new ones to the top. "Simply stunning, Zader. You're an artist, and a very, very talented one!"

"No," I blurted. "I'm not an artist. Artists make money. I just like to doodle."

"You never heard of a starving artist, then," she said. She picked up the latest drawing of Dream Girl. In it we were flying over a field of red and yellow grass with blades like octopus tentacles and flowers like furry orange caterpillars.

"This isn't doodling, Zader. Art like this belongs in the Young Artists Showcase competition. Hasn't anyone ever told you that before?"

I shrugged.

"HISAs were a couple of weeks ago. You did well on the practice tests. But I've felt like we needed something more."

The HISAs, Hawaii Independent Schools Achievement tests, were a set of tests most Hawaii private schools used as entrance exams. Ms. Robinson had drilled us on the material daily for weeks. "You want me to stay after school?" I thought of the additional hours of studying and sighed.

She laughed out loud, a deep belly laugh that I didn't think teachers made. "Oh, Zader," she said. "Yes, I want you to stay after school, but not to drill on fractions or grammar. We're going to get a portfolio together for you. You're going to enter the Young Artist Showcase competition! Don't you know what all this is?"

"No," I said, confused.

"Your ticket into Ridgemont Preparatory Academy!"

17

Uncle Kahana's Shopping List

~Luau: a Hawaiian celebration feast.~

E ven over the music on the radio I couldn't help hearing Uncle Kahana's voice through the dining room window as I came up the stairs/

"Yeah, you're right, Ilima, I think we need more purple yams," said Uncle Kahana. "Rudy and his crew like them more than poi. And we better make sure we order extra breadfruit. The painting and wrapping crews are always 'ono for baked breadfruit with butter."

Ilima chuffed.

"No worries, sistah! I already told you I'm making choke kalua pork and chicken long rice. I know how Nick and Mrs. C. love salty roast pig and fresh fish. We're serving more than fruit and veggies!"

Ilima whined.

"Now what?"

She whined again.

"Really? After all this time you're still scared of flying? How many times do I have to tell you that it was an accident? Don never—"

I heard dog nails scratch along the wooden floor, then one sharp bark at the door.

"Zader? Fo'real?" Uncle Kahana asked, then opened the door. I stood there for a second, hand in the air as Ilima tumbled out. She sniffed my toes and around my knees and licked at my fingertips.

"Howzit, Uncle Kahana," I said and scratched Ilima beneath her chin. "Good girl, Ilima."

"Aloha, Zader. Come in, come in."

I flipped off my slippahs and bent down to set them neatly outside the door and dumped my umbrella on top. "Pau, Ilima, no more kisses!" I said when she stuck her cold nose in my ear. "Uggghhh!" I shuddered. "You're giving me chicken skin!"

She snickered—I swear she did.

"Want a drink?" Uncle Kahana asked. "You can run downstairs to Hari's and make a sprunch."

"Nah, Uncle, I'm fine." I straightened up. "Uh, unless you want one?" I said.

He shook his head, gesturing at the kitchen table. "Got one already, 64-ounce opu buster. Already going 5-4-4 every five minutes."

I shut the front door as Uncle Kahana walked over to the kitchen table, picked up his drink, and took a big slurp. "You sure you don't want one?" he asked.

"No. Mahalo, though."

He gestured at the fridge, its front covered in old graduation pictures and Christmas cards. "You like noodles? I got leftover chow fun from Hari's. Still fresh."

"No, thanks. I'm here because Mom sent me."

"Oh? She likes cold chow fun?"

I laughed. "Probably. But she wanted me to make sure you knew to come over to our house on Christmas." I felt a cold nose push against my calf. I looked down. "You, too, of course, Ilima."

Ilima grinned. Fo'real, a doggy grin. She wagged her tail and lay down on her pillow.

"That's real nice of Liz to invite us; tell her mahalo plenny, yeah? But I already have plans for Christmas Day."

"You say that every year."

"That's because I have plans every year. Look." He held up a shopping list. "This year it's my turn—"

Ilima chuffed and raised her head.

"Our turn, mine and Ilima's, to plan the menu. Check it out. I'm going to cook an authentic Hawaiian Christmas luau!"

"Luau? For how many people?"

"About a hundred guests."

One hundred!

I looked around the tiny apartment and kitchen, eyebrow raised.

Uncle Kahana laughed. "Not here! At a private beach. They're going to have the imu already set up and hot and all the ingredients shipped in. I just gotta give them a shopping list. They have a big open air kitchen all set up—it's real nice. Everybody pitches in, so I figure we'll let the imu cook all Christmas Day. When it's pau, everybody'll help pound the poi, shred the meat, talk story—good times."

"Where's this beach?"

His eyes slid away. "Private," he said.

He's hiding something!

"Where? North shore side?" I pressed.

"No." He scratched his arm.

Hohonukai? Where my family comes from? Is that it?

"Where—"

"I need your opinion, Zader. This is first time I'm planning the dinner!" He proudly waved his shopping list in front of my nose. "What do you think of the menu?"

I took it and started to read. "Kalua pig, poi, purple yams, steamed breadfruit—why did you cross out salmon and write tomato next to lomi lomi?"

He gestured for me to take a seat. "Some of the folks coming don't eat meat," he said. "I thought I'd skip the salmon and just make lomi lomi tomato."

"Buddhists?"

"No, most are Christian. Although now that I think about it, probably a few free spirits and pagans, too. The main thing is some guests can't eat meat."

I narrowed my eyes. "Can't or don't?"

He pulled the list out of my fingers. "What does it matter to you? Why're you so niele?"

I looked down at the table. There was a crumb of something left over from breakfast near the shoyu bottle.

I reached out and crushed it with my fingertip, dragged it to the edge of the table, and flicked it off onto the floor. Ilima stood up from her pillow, walked over, and licked it up, giving me stink eye for making a mess. She retired to her pillow and flopped down, her back to me now.

Tell him.

"I can't eat raw fish or bloody meat," I whispered.

Uncle Kahana sat back in his chair, nodding. "That's right. Your allergies." Suddenly remembering, he spotted the water ring from his drink. He grabbed a napkin from the holder and mopped it up. "Sorry." He wiped down the sides of his cup and set it on the crumpled napkin. "What're you thinking, Zader?"

I didn't meet his eyes. "I know all the guys you know."

Uncle Kahana tilted his head, opened his mouth, shut it, closed his eyes, then tried again. "No, Zader, you don't," he said. "I get choke friends from long before you were born."

Maybe a couple old military buddies, but no one from around here and certainly not one hundred people!

"Does this private beach have a name?" I asked.

He sighed. "Yes. It's called Respite Beach."

"Respite Beach? That's out past Yokohama?"

"No. It's not on Oahu." Uncle Kahana reached out and touched my hand. "It's not your Hohonukai ohana, Zader."

I flinched. He grabbed my whole hand.

"Zader, these guys and I go way back, way back to my hanabata days when I was much younger than you. My daddy used to bring me with him. It's only been in the last ten years or so that I've been invited to come back. We get together every Christmas Day. After working through the night, they pick me and Ilima up at Keikikai beach very early in the morning and they bring us back home very late Christmas night. It's the one day they have off all year."

One day off a year? Isn't that illegal?

I opened my mouth to speak. "But—"

"No, Zader. That's it. Pau. I shouldn't have said that much."

Uncle Kahana released my hand and tapped the top of the table. The song on the radio switched to Jawaiian reggae. Uncle Kahana started humming along.

"Eh, Zader, you think those guys on the radio know they're Hawaiian, not Jamaican? Same dark skin, palm trees, and white sand beaches. Plenny tourists visit their islands, too. Different oceans, but. It's easy to confuse." He took another sip of his sprunch, rattling the ice. "You sure you don't want a soda?"

"No, thanks."

"Okay. So go tell your mother I'm fine." Ilima lifted one ear. "I mean, Ilima and I are fine. We have plans and prior commitments for Christmas Day. Mahalo for the invitation. I'll try stop by the house Christmas Eve and see everybody then."

I was drawing circles with my finger on the tabletop.

"Maybe I'll bring leftovers to you guys the day after Christmas. Liz likes her poi a little sour."

Moving my finger around and around, like suns, like bubbles, circles and spirals, rising—

"You think? I know Liz-dem loves those haupia cakes with the—"

—growing as they rise, air too thin, around and around—

Hard bump. Uncle Kahana's hand on my shoulder.

"Eh, Z-boy! Where are you?"

"Huh?"

"That's it. I'm getting some kaukau into you." Uncle Kahana stood up, grabbed a new piece of paper, and started to write. "Ilima," he said, "I need you to take this down to Hari. Z-boy, you want potato-mac or tossed salad?"

"Uh, mac salad. But Uncle, there's no need."

"Yes, need," he snapped. "How many times do I have to tell you? You gotta eat often, every two, three hours! No longer! Bumbai you're gonna drift off." Ilima stood waiting at Uncle Kahana's feet. "I'm ordering you Hari's special. Today it's a chicken katsu plate with extra mac salad. Should be ready real soon."

"Thanks, but I don't need—"

Uncle Kahana gave me stink eye. "What you said?"

"I'm not—"

"Wanna try again?"

Worse than Mom!

"Thanks, Uncle Kahana," I mumbled.

"That's better. Now, Ilima can't carry fountain drinks—"

"It's okay, I'll drink water."

"Funny," said Uncle Kahana, "so funny I forgot to laugh. I have a couple of cans of Hawaiian Sun in the icebox. Here, Ilima." He folded the note and bent down to give it to her.

She barked once, short and sharp.

Uncle Kahana shook the note. "Of course, I told Hari. But only one biscuit. You keep eating those like potato chips, bumbai you going come momona."

Ilima lowered her ears and gave one more sharp staccato bark.

"Eh," said Uncle Kahana, rubbing his nose, "I'm not the one afraid Rudy's going to drop me!"

Miffed, Ilima stood on her hind legs and swiped the note out of Uncle Kahana's hand. Nose and tail in the air, she walked to the door, waiting for Uncle Kahana to open it. When he did, she still didn't acknowledge him and daintily pranced down the stairs.

"Women!" he muttered, leaving the door open a crack.

Tell him now, I thought, *or forget about it and sit and talk story about the weather.*

Uncle Kahana cleared his throat. "Uh, nice day today."

"Yeah," I said. "Sunny. Clear."

"Good beach day."

"Yeah."

"You going to watch Jay surf later?" Uncle Kahana asked.

That's it; that's the opening. Now or never.

I shook my head. "Can't."

"What? Why? You lost your waders? Or are they leaking? You can duct tape cracks, you know." Uncle Kahana started to rummage in the junk drawer.

"It's not that." I took a deep breath. "It's Jay. He stopped surfing."

Uncle Kahana's eyes popped, eyebrows fleeing to the

top of his head. He paused, then rubbed his temples. "The shark," he said. I nodded. "Nili-boy taught you guys how to make ti leaf leis, right?"

"Yeah. Jay has one in the freezer."

"So?"

I shrugged. "He's still scared. Says he feels like shark bait floating on a platter."

Uncle Kahana blew his breath out in one great whoosh and sank into the couch. He hugged a pillow to his chest. "I'm telling you, Zader, the whole world is full of things to be scared of. For Jay, sharks should be way down on the bottom of the list."

"Shark Week reruns," I said.

"What?"

"Discovery Channel, twenty-four seven."

"For crying out loud. Fo'real?"

I nodded.

"And how many Shark Week shows are about attacks in Hawaii, hah? Who cares about California and Australia and Africa? How many times have Jay and his friends surfed here in Hawaii nei and nobody lost a leg? He's seen sharks out there before. I know that reef. One in ten fish out there is a shark. There's a shark nursery off Piko Point, for Pete's sake!"

"I think the shark he saw was big. Jaws big."

Uncle Kahana sighed and rubbed his chin. "Big shark, little shark, even the kind of shark doesn't matter. Only the nature of the shark matters. Niuhi or not. Man-eater or not. Truth: a small Niuhi can make you make die dead as easily as a big one."

"Size doesn't matter?" I asked.

He shook his head. "Not this time," a faint smile on his face. "And the lei? What about wearing a lei?"

"Jay says it could fall off."

"Tie 'em more tight."

I shrugged.

"What?"

I shrugged again.

"What?"

I didn't want to say.

Uncle Kahana raised one eyebrow. "Oh," he said. "Jay doesn't believe."

I bit my lip and looked down at the table.

No Jay doesn't. No matter what anyone says.

"Okay. So what's his problem?" Uncle Kahana asked.

"Jay doesn't understand how a ti leaf lei can keep a shark from biting."

Uncle Kahana chuckled. "Jay has a lot to learn about sharks. Sharks can do choke stuffs people don't understand." He looked at me. I looked at the table. "Right?" I didn't answer. "Right?" he asked again.

I flicked away an imaginary crumb, miserable.

I just want Jay to surf again.

Uncle Kahana put the throw pillow on the floor and leaned forward, elbows on his knees, hands hanging down. "Zader," he said. "Look at me." I raised my eyes to meet

Uncle Kahana's. He didn't flinch. "Guys who study sharks know they're special. Sharks don't get cancer or sunburn. They can track a trail of blood to its source from the tiniest manini drop. They can live a really long time. Through observation, scientists know some of the things sharks can do, but they don't know how or why." He clasped his hands together. "So why is it so hard to believe that a shark can see a ti leaf lei and not to bite?"

"If ti leaves are that powerful, how come nobody uses 'em all the time? Why don't people tie 'em on shark cages or make shark repellent spray out of ti leaves? People could just spray ti leaves on like sunscreen and pau worry about sharks."

Let him get out of that.

Uncle Kahana squished his eyes tight and rubbed his temples again. "Too much book-smart, you! Open your ears and listen. A ti leaf lei protects you. Lei, manmade for a purpose, not just ti leaves you ground up and slathered on like some anti-shark mosquito spray. Nothing about ti leaves themselves repels sharks. If you attract sharks by chumming the water with blood and fish guts and the sharks come, you better understand that you rang a dinner bell. They're hungry! If you toss fish wrapped in ti leaves into water teeming with hungry sharks they are going to gobble anything they can bite without a single thought. But we're not talking about common sharks, Z-boy. We're talking about Niuhi sharks. Niuhi sharks are special. It's not a mindless food frenzy with them; they can *reason* and *choose. A ti leaf lei sends a signal to Niuhi sharks; it iden-tifies you as—"*

The door swung open revealing Ilima carrying a plas-tic bag in her mouth. "Ah, Ilima," said Uncle Kahana. She paused halfway through the door, sensing something wasn't quite right, tilting her head as though listening to something faint and far away. She cut her eyes at me, then Uncle Kahana, then with a doggy shrug, trotted over and laid the bag at my feet.

"Thanks, Ilima." I picked up the bag and set it on the table. Inside was a pair of wooden chopsticks, napkin, and dog biscuit on top of a foil-wrapped paper plate. Peeling back a corner of the foil. I saw it was brimming with chicken katsu, sticky white rice, and potato-mac salad. I tossed the biscuit to Ilima, lifted the plate out, and set it down on the table.

Can't wait.

I snapped the chopsticks, separating them into two and sliding them back and forth, smoothing them over. I started to load them up with the first bite when I remembered my manners. Hard as it was, I set them aside.

"Uncle, you want some?" I asked. "There's too much here for me."

"Nah. All that's for you, Z-boy. I know you can grind 'em."

Score!

I shoved a massive piece of chicken into my mouth.

Heaven.

Uncle Kahana got up from the couch and opened the fridge. "There's guava juice and . . . guava. That's it." He grabbed a can, wrapped it in a paper towel and plastic bag, popped the top, and set it next to my plate.

The chicken was 'ono, golden and crisp on the outside, and the dipping sauce was sweet and gingery with a hint of garlic. I stuffed my mouth full eat, eat, eating chicken, rice, and salad until my opu could hold no more. I was always this way. I didn't feel hungry until that first bite and then it was like I hadn't eaten for a week. I couldn't get enough until suddenly I couldn't swallow another bite. I sat back in my chair, guava juice can in my hand.

"See. Told you," Uncle Kahana said. "There not even one mac noodle left." He chuckled. "'Ono?"

"Yeah?"

"Better?"

"Yeah. Mahalo, Uncle."

He flapped a hand at me. "No worries, Z-boy. I remember what it was like to be eleven and growing."

He motioned to the plate. "Pau?"

"Yeah."

"Good. I'm tossing it in the rubbish, then." He picked up the litter from the table, tucked it in the garbage can under the kitchen sink, and tied the trash bag closed. "Bumbai I'll take 'em outside. I don't want cockroaches in here." He shuddered. "Don't get me started on the flying kine. Bamboocha!"

I turned the juice can around in my hands, watching the

way the light played over the pink and green label through the plastic.

Ask him. You need to know so you can make Jay understand.

"Uncle," I started.

"Yeah," he said.

"You were saying about ti leaves and leis. Do you mean that when sharks spot the lei they won't bite?"

Uncle Kahana sat down across the table from me, taking the can from my hands and lifting my chin. "Here's the secret, Zader, and you can't tell Jay. He's scared enough about sharks already. Ti leaf leis don't prevent Niuhi sharks from biting. Nothing can keep a Niuhi shark from biting you once he decides to bite. Ti leaf leis simply remind Niuhi sharks of their manners. It's still the shark's choice to bite or not."

"So if Niuhi shark wants to bite—"

"Nothing you can do."

"Stay out of the water," I said.

Ilima chuffed and stuck out her tongue, grinning again.

"Kulikuli, Ilima," Uncle Kahana said. "Mind your own beeswax."

Ilima walked over and put her head on my knee. I rubbed her ears. "Jay can't stay out of the water," I said. "He thinks he can, but he can't."

"Jay needs the ocean like—"

"Air," I said. "This is the longest he's been out of the ocean since he got chicken pox. Probably since we were old enough to go beach by ourselves. We gotta get him back surfing. Now all he wants to do is watch the Discovery Channel."

"First thing, turn off the TV," Uncle Kahana said.

"An'den?"

"An'den, I dunno. Let me think about it for a while. Jay knows sharks don't like to eat people, right? I mean, people taste real pilau to sharks—any kind of shark, not just Niuhi sharks."

"How come?"

Uncle Kahana shrugged. "I heard it's because we taste like mud."

"Mud? How do you know that?"

Uncle Kahana looked up, startled. "I dunno. Maybe I heard it on Shark Week."

"How? You don't have cable."

"I have ways," Uncle Kahana said, wagging his eyebrows.

"What do you mean?"

"I know what those shark guys say."

"One Shark Week guy said sharks are valuable. Their liver oil, fins, cartilage, stuffs li'dat can help people—"

"Whoa. Just cool your jets one minute. You gotta promise me right now, Zader, that you'll never, ever eat shark. Ever. I mean it."

"Okay."

"Fo'real. No shark meat ever." Uncle Kahana glowered.

"Okay."

"Promise," he growled.

"I just did!"

Uncle Kahana looked at his hands and ran one thumbnail under the other. "Okay," he said. "Good."

"Uncle Kahana, this thing with Niuhi sharks. Is it an 'aumakua thing?"

"No. Yes." He sat there thinking for a minute. "Not really. Not 'aumakua. Kinda, but not. Just don't eat shark and don't hassle them. Respect."

"Like 'aumakua."

"Fine," he sighed. "Like 'aumakua. Heaven help us," he muttered.

"On one Shark Week show, this guy did experiments. He made a cutout of a surfer on a board and chummed the water. He said big sharks bite surfers because they think they're turtles or seals or something else. Not people."

"Something else, hah?" said Uncle Kahana, a little distractedly. "Tell me, was this guy was studying big sharks or big Niuhi sharks? If he didn't know he was studying Niuhi sharks, maybe they were just pulling his leg. Mistaken identity's an easy answer, right? No blame, just honest confusion in the heat of the moment. They can hide in plain sight."

"Who's hiding?" I asked.

"You ever bite a tree thinking it was a hamburger when you were super hungry, Zader? You ever seen Ilima gnaw on a chair leg thinking it was a bone?"

"Ah, no . . ."

"Ti leaf lei, no ti leaf lei. Sometimes it's personal."

His eyes were unfocused looking far into the past, somewhere I couldn't follow. I touched his arm. "Uncle

Kahana, you want something to eat? I can heat up some chow fun noodles."

"What? Oh, no, no, Z-boy. I was just thinking. Jay's got nothing personal there. The shark thing is all in his head."

"What's personal?"

"Hah? Nothing. Jay has no reason to be scared. We just gotta convince him of that."

I WAS HEADING HOME WHEN I heard the music—soft and sweet—coming from behind the Kanahele's fence.

'Ukulele, I thought. *Somebody having a party?*

I peeked over the fence and almost make die dead right there on the dirt. Sitting under the mango tree and strumming with a voice like heaven itself was Tunazilla. Next to her was a hammajang teddy bear, half the fuzz gone and missing one eye. I stood there, jaw on the ground, unable to believe those sounds, rich like butterscotch cream and smoother than honey, were coming from that mouth.

"Eh, Tuna-head! Tutu wants you to come inside and make the rice."

I ducked behind the fence.

Please don't let him see me!

"What're you doing out here, hah? Singing? You're scaring the birds," Alika taunted.

"Shut-up, Alika," said Tunazilla. "Don't call me Tuna-head."

"Tunazilla, then. Go wash the rice."

"When I go Ridgemont next year, you won't talk to me like that," Tuna said.

"Ridgemont? Yeah, right. No way they're gonna let a monster like you in there. You'd just ugly up the place."

"Ms. Robinson said I have a chance."

"Yeah, you have a chance, j'like I have a chance. Everybody has a chance."

"Ms. Robinson said mine was fo'real."

"And you believed her? That's how I know you don't have a chance. You're stupid, Tunazilla. Always gonna be. Ugly, too. J'like your bear."

"Leave him alone, Alika."

"Or what?"

"You put him down or bumbai you gonna find out."

I didn't stay and I didn't find out. I put my head down and ran for home thinking for the first time I was glad to be me.

18
MAKING LEIS

~Pupule: crazy; reckless; insane.~

I came in the house through the front door leaving my slippahs and umbrella outside. Jay was sitting in front of the TV eyes glazed as a great white shark flipped a seal around and around in the air before crushing it in its jaws.

"Eh," he said as I crossed between him and the TV. "You see that, Zader?"

I ignored him and continued on my way to the voices in the back.

Wow. Looks like a rainforest bomb exploded!

Lili, Mele, Char Siu, and Mom were sitting at the kitchen table sorting through tangles of vines, flowers, and stems. Punkin was standing at the sink shaking water off ferns, and Aunty Amy was wrapping finished leis in plastic bags and setting them in a cooler on the floor.

"Watch out, Zader," Mom said.

"Yeah," said Aunty Amy, "I think there's water over here on the floor."

I paused in the doorway. "What's the scoop?"

Lili sighed the way only sixteen-year-old sisters can.

"You have eyes, Zader? We're making leis for the Christmas show at Ala Moana. Our halau is dancing there next Saturday."

Punkin sniffed. "Tourists," she said. "I don't know why we gotta make all this for them. Fake flowers are good enough."

Aunty Amy flicked at dishtowel at her. "Punkin! For shame! Halau Na Pua O Lauele never, ever wears fake anything! How many times do I have to tell you girls that hula is not like soccer or Girl Scouts or jazz dance! It's a way of life, titah, and you better decide if you want to be part of it or not!"

"Hummphh!" said Punkin, bringing an armful of freshly washed ferns to the table. "I like to dance. I like to perform. I don't even mind it too much when Kumu drones on and on about the kaona of the hula or the oli. I just hate making leis! It's itchy!" She scratched at her wrist and scowled.

"Did you talk with Uncle Kahana?" Mom asked.

"Yeah. He said he already has plans with friends for Christmas."

"Bulai! What friends?" Mom said.

"I dunno. He said from his hanabata days."

Mom snorted. "As if."

"He said this year it was his turn to cook." I picked up an escaping flower from the floor and threw it on the table.

"Uncle Kahana cooks?" Char Siu asked. "Huh. I thought he always ate at Hari's."

"He said he's cooking a Christmas luau for one hundred people." I leaned against the doorframe. "His turn."

Mom shook her head. "Amy, it's like I told you. He's getting more and more pupule every day. Talking to himself. Puttering around the reef and docks with that dog. Now he thinks he's cooking a Christmas luau for one hundred people. As if he even knows one hundred people to invite!" Mom shoved broken stems and brown petals into a rubbish bag, sweeping the table clean. "He needs help."

I cleared my throat. "No, Mom; it's okay. Uncle Kahana said he'll have plenny help. There's a big kitchen and imu already on the beach and everything."

"What imu on the beach? Where?" Mom's eyes were like lasers. I was in trouble, but I didn't know why. Typical.

I shrugged. "Private, he said. Not even on Oahu."

Mom gathered the top of the rubbish bag and whipped it around and around her hand, twisting it closed. "Not on Oahu? And how does he think he's getting there? Flap his wings and fly?"

I rubbed at something on my arm. "Boat, maybe. He said they're picking him up early at Keikikai beach."

She tossed the rubbish bag next to the cooler. "Bubbles. That old man is talking bulai and bubbles! There's no place to dock a boat at Keikikai—they'd have to beach it! People with boats big enough to sail inter-island dock at Lauele Harbor. Why not meet at the harbor?" She looked around. "Well?" All the girls got busy tying and sorting. "I'll tell you why. It's because there is no imu on a private beach, no luau, no one hundred people! Just one skinny stubborn Hawaiian kanaka who doesn't want to come to my house

Christmas Day. Easter, sure. New Year's, fine. Birthdays, always. But not Christmas!"

Aunty Amy said, "Relax, Liz. Every year he disappears on Christmas. Maybe he needs to be alone."

"Nobody needs to be alone on Christmas!"

"Maybe he does."

"I don't like it. Family should be together on Christmas."

"He said he'd come by Christmas Eve," I said.

Mom just snorted again and raised an eyebrow. I knew this wasn't over.

"Liz, look at this," said Aunty Amy. She was holding up a long, open-ended lei. "This is the new style I was telling you about. Looks like maile, yeah?" She turned the lei around so Mom could see it from the table. "This is what I want the boys to wear when they do their hapa-haole number. Aunty Harriett showed me how to make it out of ti leaves. Not as nice as maile, but way cheaper. What do you think?" She handed the lei to Mom.

"Beautiful," said Mom. "And easy to make them the right length. What did Tomas and Micah think?"

Aunty Amy shrugged. "They picked the ti leaves for me readily enough," she said, giving Punkin small kine stink eye. "I think they like them."

Mom held out the lei for Aunty Amy to place in the cooler. The light from the kitchen window was shining behind it, outlining the patterns and shapes of the lei as it hung suspended in air.

"Zader, are you okay?" Char Siu asked. "You're looking funny kine."

"How can you tell?" snarked Punkin.

"Shut up, Punkin," said Lili. "Leave my brother alone."

"Zader," said Mom. "You okay? You didn't get any water on you, did you?"

I shook my head, scattering the shadows and lines of the lei from my vision. "No, no—just did anybody see Nili-boy today?"

Mele tossed her hair back. "Probably surfing. The waves were pretty good today at Nalupuki."

Char Siu glanced out the window. "Sun's going down soon. Better hurry if you wanna catch him."

Mele giggled. "If you miss him at the beach, just look for Nalani."

Aunty Amy smiled. "I've seen the way he looks at her. Those puppy eyes! Worse than Ilima!"

"I thought she was dating Kawika Choy," said Punkin.

"Oh, Nili-boy's much better," said Lili.

"Hotter," Char Siu said.

"Char Siu!" Aunty Amy said.

"Oh, Mom, you know what I mean," Char Siu said.

"No," said Aunty Amy. "I think we need to discuss it."

The girls all groaned, but I caught the wink Aunty Amy gave Mom.

I turned to go. "Zader," Mom called, "take Jay with you."

I frowned. Taking Jay with me was definitely going to cramp my style. Mom caught my eye and gave me her "don't argue" look.

I eased back into the living room. "Jay," I said, "wanna go check out the waves at Nalupuki? I need to find Nili-boy."

He looked at me from the couch, head resting on a pillow and watching TV sharks bite and blood foam on the water. "Did you know more surfers die from shark bites than jellyfish stings?"

"So?"

"Don't forget your umbrella!" called Mom.

I winced and grabbed the hated thing from its place by the door. "So?" I repeated.

"You know how many times I've gotten stung by jellyfish?" He rubbed his nose. "Too many times to count."

"So?"

Jay rolled his eyes. "You just don't get it. It's just a matter of time, brah. We're all shark bait out there."

"What're you saying, Jay?"

He waved his arms and legs like a marionette. "Dangling legs and arms. Pupus on a platter, brah. Shark bait."

"You carry meat tenderizer?" I asked.

"What?"

"Meat tenderizer? You have some?"

"Yeah. In my surf bag."

"Why?" I asked.

"For jellyfish, you lolo! Takes the sting out. Everybody knows that." He tucked his hand under his chin.

"You have a ti leaf lei?" I said.

"Yeah. In the freezer."

"So? Meat tenderizer—ti leaf lei. It's all the same. Wear the lei like Nili-boy said and get back in the water."

"Zader, do you know what a ti leaf is to sharks?" asked Jay. "Garnish."

I shook my head at him. "Whatever. Mom, I'm going!" I called.

"What about Jay?" she yelled.

"I'm staying," he hollered. He sat up and looked at me with his sad surfer eyes. "Shark bait. You wait. It's all just a matter of time."

19
THE PLAN

Kahuna: priest; sorcerer; an expert.

Nili-boy was already tying his board to the roof of his car when I got to the beach. He had an old beach towel wrapped around his hips and his hair was spiky from the salt. I wandered over and lean against his hood.

"Howzit, Little Cuz," he said, "where's Jay? Long time since I've seen him out there."

"Home. Shark Week reruns."

"Ah." Nili-boy adjusted the last strap on the rack, tightening it down for the drive back to Waimanalo. "That's bad."

I nodded. "Couple of weeks ago I think a shark psyched Jay out."

"Ti leaf lei?"

I shook my head. "He doesn't believe."

Nili-boy crossed his arms and leaned his 'okole against the driver's door. "He's scared to surf," said Nili-boy. "Plenny guys quit after seeing something like that." He looked out at the ocean watching a set roll in.

I chose my words carefully. "Uncle Kahana said there's

only one kind of shark to worry about. Niuhi shark. The kine that eats men."

Nili-boy lifted his chin to the ocean. "He's right. Niuhi is the only kind that eats people. All the other sharks avoid us. You know Niuhi can look like any kind of shark, right? It's the nature, not the type of shark that makes it Niuhi. I've seen plenny regular sharks out there, mostly small ones. Niuhi is rare—super rare. To get bit, not only do you have to come across a Niuhi shark, but it's also gotta be a super hungry Niuhi shark." He shrugged. "I figure I have a better chance at winning a trillion-dollar lottery."

"Nili-boy, Uncle Kahana told me the Niuhi shark chooses."

He raised an eyebrow at me. "He did?"

"Yeah. He said with Jay it's not personal."

Nili-boy laughed, "Uncle Kahana said that?" I nodded. "Fo'real? He said that?"

I nodded again.

Nili-boy wiped an eye. "Well, I guess he would know," he said. "Being a shark kahuna and all."

Is Nili-boy teasing? I tilted my head toward him.

"What you do you think?"

"Can you imagine Uncle Kahana to hosting Shark Week?"

I just looked at him, still unsure.

"Nah, you're right, Zader. No matter how pupule people think he is, Uncle Kahana knows more about sharks, especially Niuhi sharks, in these waters than any scientist. If he says the Niuhi shark chooses, the shark chooses. And if it's not personal, then Jay's got nothing to worry about. Get choke 'ono fish in the sea. Who'd want a chunk of Jay when they could have fresh ahi?"

"Uncle Kahana says it's not the ti leaf, it's the lei."

"Yeah. That's why some guys have special tattoos. Same-same as the lei," Nili-boy said. He bent down, fiddling with his slippah. Suddenly, he straightened up, slippah in hand. "Wait, Zader!" He shook his slippah at me. "You know Aunty Liz-dem going broke yo' head if you and Jay get tattoos!"

"Yeah, I know Mom would freak out."

"Good because I know who else is going to get blamed if you and Jay do something li'dat. And I like all my parts in one piece."

"Not a tattoo. I have another idea." I touched the nose of his board. "Nili-boy, how hard is it to refinish a surfboard?"

He dropped his slippah on the pavement. "Depends on the board. What're you thinking, Little Cuz?"

"I want to refinish Jay's board for Christmas and put a ti leaf lei all around the bottom. That way Jay won't worry that a Niuhi shark is going to see him and think he's a turtle or seal or—"

"Shark bait," said Nili-boy.

I nodded.

"I think you onto something akamai, Zader." Nili-boy turned and considered his board. "I have stuff to take the wax off, plus masking tape, ding filler, things like that—but you're going to need some good, fast drying acrylic spray paint and probably some paint pens."

My cigar box art kit's not going to do it. I need some real art supplies.

"Paint pens? Not magic markers, right? Where would I get those?" I asked.

He laughed. "Try Hari's, he carries everything." He tapped his board, thinking. "Lauele Surf Designs, I know those guys. Maybe they'll have some old leftover paint we can use. What colors you do you need?"

"Greens," I said. "Browns for shading, black for outlining. Maybe a cream background? What do you think?"

"You ever used a spray gun?"

"No."

"You get kala?"

"No cash. But I can work."

Nili-nodded. "Okay. I'll talk to them. Maybe I can work something out, maybe not. I'll call."

Nili-boy opened the driver's door, shook the towel from his hips, and tossed it in the back. "Pretty dry now," he said, patting his 'okole. He held out his fist for a bump. "You're a good brother, Little Cuz. Laters."

We bumped fists. "Laters," I said.

20
THE NO LETTER DAY

~Make "A": to screw up; to embarrass oneself.~

I heard Char Siu banging up the steps before I saw her. She was waving a piece of paper over her head and dancing on the lanai. Aunty Amy was walking more sedately across the street, but I could hear the happy way her slippahs were slap, slap, slapping the asphalt.

Great. Just great. I'm gonna be all alone.

"Aunty Liz! Aunty Liz! I got it! I got my letter from Ridgemont!"

I opened the door. "Zader!" She threw her arms around my neck. "I got in!" she squealed.

I patted her back. "Good for you."

"Where's Aunty Liz-dem?"

"In the kitchen."

She kicked off her slippahs and dashed through the living room to the kitchen. I waited, holding the door for Aunty Amy.

"Howzit, Zader."

"Aloha, Aunty."

She bent down and gathered Char Siu's slippahs and

lined them up neatly with her own slippahs by the side of the door. She straightened up, took one look at me, and wrapped me in a big hug. "Jay?"

I nodded.

"Oh, sweetheart." She hugged me tighter. "Maybe it's just held up in the mail."

"Doesn't matter," Jay said. "I'm not going." He'd walked in from the kitchen, Char Siu and Mom trailing behind.

"Me neither," Char Siu said. "I didn't want to get up super early to ride a bus to school anyway."

"Go to school with a bunch of private school snobs, no way," Jay said.

"Hey," said Lili coming from her bedroom, "I'm one of those private school snobs."

"See what I mean," Jay said.

"Now everybody just chillax a moment," Dad said, phone in hand. "Two kinds of letters went out yesterday, 'early acceptance' and 'we regret to inform you.' Zader didn't get either."

"So what does that mean?" asked Char Siu.

"I just spoke with Ms. Robinson. She said most private schools hold a few spots open on a waitlist while they make their final selections. She talked with the dean of admissions at Ridgemont and Zader's on the waitlist. There are five names and three open spots."

"So?"

"They're still deciding. Ms. Robinson said the all the kids on the waitlist are similar in academics. What distinguishes them are—"

"Talents," said Jay.

"Art," said Char Siu.

"The show," I said.

Dad nodded. "Ms. Robinson said she made sure the admissions dean from Ridgemont knew your art was in the Young Artist Showcase."

"I didn't win."

"Your turtle carving got honorable mention," Mom said.

"I didn't win."

"The age range was all the way through high school," said Aunty Amy. "You're in sixth grade. You weren't supposed to win."

"I was supposed to get into Ridgemont. Make 'A.'"

"No, no, no! You didn't make 'A,' Zader! You're going Ridgemont next year. You will," said Lili. "Trust me."

21
Hohonukai Cousin

~Honi: to kiss, to greet in the traditional Hawaiian style,; nose to nose,
exchanging breath.~

"I already told you, Ilima, there aren't big 'opihi Keikikai side of the rocks, only manini kine! We gotta go way out past Yokohama to find those big buggers you like."

Ilima chuffed, skirting around an empty crab shell, bright orange against the black lava rocks. The ocean spray splashed against the cold lava, blowing salt kisses in the afternoon breeze. Kahana shifted his bucket from one hand to the other. "Besides, we're just checking things out right now. It's still too early to pick limu for the Christmas luau."

Ilima pricked her ears and turned toward Piko Point. She stood on her hind legs, then gave a sharp bark.

"What? Another crab?" grumbled Kahana. He turned to look at her. Ilima's tail was wagging and her eyes were bright and locked on Piko Point. He followed her gaze to see a young woman in a tourist print sarong worn in the old kikepa style standing next to Pohaku. Running away from the woman and toward the beach was the slim figure of a barefooted girl in a too-big sun dress.

"Oh, confunit," said Kahana.

When the girl hit the sand and started running up the beach, the woman turned toward them and waved. "Double-confunit with kukae on the side," he said. He grinned from ear to ear and waved back, faking it. He turned away a little, hiding his sigh. "Okay, Ilima let's go. But you better mind your manners," he warned. He tilted his head at Ilima, considering. "Maybe it's better if you stay over here with the bucket and wait. We don't have a lei and—"

Ilima whined and rubbed her nose with her paw.

"What about Lassie, ah?" said Kahana. "If you come, who's going to be the hero and call for help when I'm stuck in the well?"

With a doggy rumble in her throat, Ilima lay down, head on her front paws and nose toward the woman in the distance. Kahana rubbed her yellow head. "Good girl," he said.

Ilima closed her eyes, then opened one eye with a sniff.

"Believe me, Ilima," said Kahana, "I would trade you places in a heartbeat." He set down the bucket and turned toward the woman standing by Pohaku. "Remember," he muttered to Ilima, "one bark for land, two barks for sea."

Ilima chuffed, licked her lips, and settled down to watch.

Kahana squared his shoulders, hitched up his shorts, and started out to the point. "Eh, Cousin!" he called as he climbed over and around the lava.

"Cousin," she called back, then turned away and squatted down next to the large saltwater pool.

As Kahana approached he noticed his spear-fishing

bag—neatly folded—was sitting on the lava next to Pohaku. The woman had her back to Kahana, the folds of her kikepa falling gracefully over her shoulder. She was doing something in the water: splashing, turning, and lifting. Kahana tried not to flinch when she pivoted on the balls of her feet and gently laid a gleaming chunk of ahi still seeping blood and seawater on top of the bag. She spun back to the salt pool and rinsed the fish scales and blood from her hands, flicking the drops to the middle of the pool. She spoke to the water.

"Le'ia and I wanted to thank you for your gift of fish the other day," she said. "It was 'ono, very fresh." She stood and faced him.

"Ka-Pua-O-Ke-Kai," whispered Kahana.

"Kahana, of the Lauele Kaulupali ohana," said Pua. "Long time." She held her arms out. "What? No honi for your Hohonukai cousin?"

"Of course, of course," stammered Kahana as he stumbled closer for her embrace. He placed his hands on her shoulders and pressed his nose to her nose. He closed his eyes, exhaled, and then slowly inhaled the sweet salt smell of her breath. Her skin was ocean chilled to the touch and slightly raspy with salt. He pulled back a little and looked into her eyes, so dark and flat, just like her son's.

"Aloha, Kahana," she said, pointing to her chest. "I carry you always."

"Aloha, Pua," said Kahana, "and I, you."

She gestured to the beach. "I sent Le'ia to find some

banana leaves to wrap the tuna in. I thought that might make it easier to carry."

Kahana bowed his head. "Mahalo nui loa for the fish, Cousin. It's beautiful. Ilima and I will eat well tonight." He paused. "You and your daughter will join us?"

Eyes on the beach, she shook her head. "Mahalo for the invitation," she said, "but we've already eaten." She glanced back at the gleaming chunk of prime ahi, sliced with surgical precision from the belly of a much larger fish.

Kahana nodded. "It's good to see you," he said.

"But why am I here?" Pua laughed. "You're right. Pohaku could have watched the ahi until you came. He is a good go-between, is he not?" She smiled and moved to sit next to the aumakua rock, tucking her feet behind her. "He's happy to have a purpose again, I think." She patted the lava. "Come. Sit."

Kahana glanced back at Ilima, a blond spot next to an old bucket against a black lava sea. He rolled his shoulders, hitched up his shorts again, and sat down.

"Zader's birthday gifts," said Kahana.

"What?" She blinked. Kahana held his breath, confused. "Gifts for the boy?" said Pua slowly.

Kahana sensed danger in the shallow reef in the sea of manners he was navigating. "Your pardon, Cousin. Each year around the date of Zader's birth, here, next to Pohaku, I've found an offering, a gift I thought—"

"Ah." Pua smiled. "Yes, those are from me." Kahana slowly let the trapped air ease out of his lungs. "But they aren't for the boy," she said. "They are for his—for Elizabeth Mapuana."

"Liz?"

"Yes. To thank her for doing what I cannot. I owe her."

"Liz thinks—we thought—the gifts were for Zader. For his future."

"His future?" She turned her cold, flat eyes to Kahana's. Holding his breath again, he managed not to flinch. "His future does not need treasures from me."

"Liz is afraid you'll take him back."

Pua closed her eyes and tipped her head to the afternoon sun. She eased up slowly, brushing imaginary sand off her kikepa. "She has nothing to fear from me. He will make his own choices in his own time."

Kahana watched the emotions play across her face.

I'm glad I left Ilima with the bucket, he thought. *Cousin or not, I'm still not sure.*

"I saw you combing the reef. Dinner?" she asked.

"No, no, just checking things out." He shrugged. "Christmas luau, soon."

"Respite Beach," she said.

He gaped at her. "You know what goes on at Respite Beach?" he said.

She smiled. "You really need to ask?" she teased.

"You coming?"

She shook her head. "No. It's not really my crowd," she said.

Kahana nodded. "Too jolly."

"Something like that." She paused. "The boy."

"Zader."

She looked toward the shore. "His brother. The surfer."

"Jay."

She nodded. "Jay. I haven't seen him for quite a while."

Kahana sighed. "He's scared."

"He's a good surfer. Natural."

"Yes."

"Shame."

"Yes."

"Can you get him back in the water?" she asked.

"And how is your brother," Kahana asked, "Ka-Lei-O-Mano?"

Pua sighed. "Away. Taking care of family business in Hohonukai and elsewhere. Kalei has no reason to be here."

"No?"

Pua picked at the edge of her kikepa. "No." She fiddled with the ti leaf lei around her neck. It was worn and dry as if stored too long in a cool, dry place. "No," she said again. "That is long in the past. He understands now that your father was helping."

"Good," said Uncle Kahana. "I don't want Jay blamed for things that happened long before he was born."

She lifted the lei from around her neck and looped it over and over her wrist, the dry leaves crackling. "Jay knows about ti leaf leis?"

"Nili-boy showed him." Kahana ran a hand through his hair. "He doesn't believe."

"That is a problem," she said.

"Zader—"

"I prefer Kaonakai."

Kahana dipped his head. "Kaonakai has an idea."

"Oh?"

"He's an artist."

She smiled a Mona Lisa smile.

He cut his eyes at her. "You knew that?"

"It doesn't surprise me."

"He wants to mark Jay's board."

"And this is better than a lei?"

"Leis fall off."

"People fall off."

"I thought you said it was nothing personal?" Kahana echoed.

"It's not," she conceded. "This is for Jay, then?"

"It is."

Pua stood. Le'ia was running back to the lava flow, banana leaves waving like banners over her head. "Get him in the water again," said Pua. "I'll make him believe."

22
THE THEFT

~Cockaroach: to steal; to swipe; to take without permission.~

The night before the hula halau's Christmas performance in Waikiki, Jay's surfboard was stolen. It'd been
propped up on our front lanai gathering dust for weeks
now. Christmas was only days away. Jay took the news with
a shrug. Shark Week reruns had lost their appeal and he'd
moved onto flag football, spending his time after school
wearing knee-high tube socks dangling over the waistband
of his pants, waiting for the pass and tackle.

"Jay, it's your board! Somebody cockaroached your
board right off the lanai. Don't you wanna do something
about it?" Char Siu said. She was standing in our driveway
and wearing too much makeup.

"Charlene, you know Halloween's over?" Jay taunted.

"Shut up! It's for the stage, lolo!"

Jay snickered.

"And don't call me Charlene! I hate it!" she said.

"Charlene Suzette! Charlene Suzette!"

"Wassa mattah you, hah? You four years old? I said don't
call me that!" Char Siu punched Jay in the shoulder.

"Owweeeeeee!" Jay wailed rubbing his arm.

"Panty!" she spat.

"Bozo!" he snapped.

"Enough!" roared Mom running down the front steps. "Both of you. In the car, now! Where's Lili?"

"She's riding with Punkin-dem. They just left, Aunty Liz." Char Siu climbed in the back. "Thanks for giving me a ride. Mom said she'll meet us with the leis by the koi fountain."

"No problem, Char Siu." Mom turned to me. "Are you sure you don't want to come? After all the performances we're going out to dinner, maybe even a movie. We're going to be back late."

"No," I said. "I feel really junk. My head hurts." I sniffed experimentally. "I think I'm catching cold."

Dad bounced down the stairs jiggling the keys. He put the back of his warm hand on my forehead. "No fever," he said. "Cool as always."

"You're never sick, Zader," said Mom.

I shrugged. "I woke with a sore stomach and a killer headache. I think I just need more sleep." I sniffed again.

"Paul?" Mom turned to Dad.

Dad shrugged. "He's old enough to stay home by himself. I don't think he'd miss a movie in Waikiki just to avoid Ala Moana's crowds, Liz. He must be sick."

"Hmmm," Mom said. "Okay, then. Drink a little juice. There's some rice leftover if your tummy's up to it. Just take it easy today."

"Okay."

"I mean it. Nothing strenuous. Don't make yourself worse."

"How about drawing? Can I draw?"

Mom reached out and patted my cheek. "Yes. Call if you need us."

"Okay."

I watched them get in the car and drive away, Char Siu and Jay still bickering in the back seat.

No wonder Lili went with Punkin.

When the car was gone, I went in the house, scrambled under my bed, and gathered my designs. Ten minutes later Nili-boy pulled up.

"Ready?"

"Yep."

"Good. Got the board prepped last night. Rad's waiting for us at the shop."

23
SURF DESIGNS

~Kokua: to help, assist, accommodate.~

When we entered Lauele Surf Designs, an old haole guy with a long scraggly blond ponytail and black pearl earring looked up from the counter where he was sorting receipts. "Eh, Nili!" he said. "What's up?"

"Howzit!" They grabbed hands surfer-style and bumped chests across the counter. "Rad," said Nili-boy, "this is my cousin, Zader."

"Howzit!" He wrapped his rough hand around mine and gave it a shake. "So you're Jay Westin's brother?" I nodded. "I watched him at the October Menehune Surf Meet at Sunset. Under twelve, yeah?" I nodded again. "He's good, really good. If he keeps it up, he can go pro." He tagged Nili-boy on the arm. "Probably do better than this guy."

"He has to get back in the water first," I said.

Rad sobered. "Nili told me a little about that. Big shark. Hard sometimes. He got bumped?"

Nili-boy shook his head. "No, no bites, nothing. He just psyched himself out."

"Shark Week?" Rad asked.

Nili-boy grinned. "Reruns 24-7."

"And you think you can help get him back in the water with a custom paint job?" Rad raised his eyebrows at me.

"Show 'em," said Nili-boy.

I opened my folder and took out a piece of paper with my designs on it.

"Wow," said Rad, "I've never seen anything like it. You drew this?"

"Yeah," I said.

"What do you think?" asked Nili-boy.

Rad whistled. "If you can paint as good as you draw, I might have a job for you. Ever use a spray gun?"

"No," I said.

Rad nodded, turning the paper around. "This is probably too complicated for a spray gun anyway. I think you better use paint pens. Last night Nili and I stripped off the old finish from Jay's board, filled the dings, sanded it smooth, and painted it a soft cream color. It's ready to go."

I looked at Nili-boy and then down at my drawing. "No worries, Cuz," he said softly. "It's Christmas. Miracles happen, yeah?"

Rad saw my dilemma. "Ah, I get it. Custom paint's expensive."

I nodded, wondering how many car washes, lawn mowings, and lanai sweepings I was in for.

"I'll let you in on a secret. Art and time are expensive. Paint, not so much." He tapped my drawing. "Truthfully, it costs a lot to get all the tools, supplies, and set up a shop, but once you have them doing one more board costs pennies—as long as someone else is doing the work."

Rad handed me back my drawings and jerked his head toward the back of the store. "Nili's right. It's Christmas. I'd hate to see a talented surfer like Jay beach himself because of a shark scare, and if you think this will help . . ." He shrugged. "Kokua, yeah, Zader? One artist to another. Just clean up after yourself, and we'll call it even. C'mon. I'll show you where you can work."

"This is where I say laters, Little Cuz," said Nili-boy. "I've got to run, but I'll be back bumbai."

"Thanks, Nili-boy," I said.

He laughed. "Don't thank me yet. Wait until you're through. It's hard work, you know." He squeezed my shoulder. "No worries. You can handle it. Laters."

And he was out the door.

"This way," said Rad.

Behind the surf shop was a covered lanai with bright portable lights like construction workers use. Jay's board lay upside down gleaming in the artificial light and resting on two saw horses. I trailed a finger over the board and bent down to examine the surface. Every ding and dent was gone, the lines pure and smooth.

It's perfect.

"The board wasn't too bad. Just some minor pukas that Nili and I filled and sanded. The base is a warm, classic cream. Nili told me your design was heavy in the greens,

and I thought the cream would make a good contrast."
He reached over and picked up a worn surfboard leash.
"I noticed the leash is getting a little hammajang. With a
new paint job, you might want to replace it." He grinned.
"I'll give you the kama'aina rate."

The board was not as shiny as it would be when the
final clear coat was on it, but it was flawless. I swallowed.

Maybe I should just leave the board alone. What if I ruin it?
What if I make it look so junk Jay won't surf because his board's
too ugly? I shook the thought off. *He's not surfing now; what's*
the difference?

Rad motioned me over to a table and adjusted the lights.
He reached behind a coffee can stuffed with pens and pencils and tugged on the end of a big a roll of butcher paper,
unwinding a long sheet across the table top. Grabbing a
couple of shoe box-sized bins off a shelf, he used them to
anchor the ends of the paper and motioned me to sit down.
I sat, feeling like I was in a doctor's office.

But am I the doctor or the patient?

Rad nudged one of the bins. "This box has greens and
the other has blacks and browns. There are other colors
over there," he vaguely motioned toward the shelf, "but I
think everything you need is here."

"Okay." I hesitated.

Where do I begin?

Rad caught the waver in my voice. "If you want, you
can start by lightly sketching your design on the board
with a pencil—"

"No." I was shocked at how firm my voice sounded, like I knew what I was doing.

Rad paused, amused.

"I mean, I'd rather freehand it, no sketching." I swallowed. "I think."

Rad really looked at me for the first time since we came out on the lanai. He nodded. "Good. That's good. Some guys like to pencil everything first. Using tape is better—no stray marks. I'll show you a trick I use when I freehand—little pieces of tape to mark my dimensions; it helps me make sure the design stays balanced."

I nodded, looking at the butcher paper. "I don't want pencil lines bleeding through the paint."

"That's usually not a problem with pen paints unless you push too hard with the pencil and make indentations." Rad picked up a pen. "This kind of paint dries really fast, but it's still better to do all of your main color first, then go back and add shadows and highlights."

He took my designs and spread them out along the top edge of the butcher paper, turning them a little in the light. "You drew this with colored pencils, right?"

I nodded.

"To make it snap on the board, you'll want to go back and outline the finished design in a fine to medium black line. Just my recommendation." I nodded again. "Practice first." Rad tapped the table. "Paint pens are different than markers or colored pencils—they feel more like dry erase pens on white boards. You have them at school?"

"Yeah," I said.

"It won't feel exactly the same—the paint will move faster on the surfboard—but try it here first. It'll give you an idea of how to control the pen. Watch your wrist and arm. It's easy to smear if you're not careful." He reached up and grabbed a roll of paper towels off a shelf. "For cleaning up," he said. "Holler if you need anything." He tossed the paint pen back into the box, gave me a knuckle bump, and turned toward the shop.

As I started to sort through the pens, I heard Rad open a cabinet and flip a switch. 'Ukulele music filled the lanai. "Jams," he said, "vital. They fill in the spaces."

He walked back to the store whistling *Guava Jelly*.

I picked up a medium green, pulled off the cap, and started to draw the basic shape of a twisted ti leaf lei. The paint flowed thick.

Too much. It needs a light touch, lighter than a regular marker.

After drawing a few more twists in the lei, the paint began to even out, the music strummed, and I drifted. Much later, I noticed a shift in the music and paused to look at my work. A beautiful lei danced across the paper.

I did that? Maybe Jay's board won't suck after all.

I was touching up the last black line when Nili-boy and Rad came out the store's back door and headed over to me.

"Wow lau lau," Nili-boy said, leaning over my shoulder. He handed me an orange Diamond Head soda. "Don't worry; it's warm."

Rad picked up my practice papers and turned them this way and that in the light. "Not bad. You figured out how to get the paint just right—not too thick or smeary. I like the way you used the metallic for the highlights here and here. You sure you never done this before?"

"No."

Rad smiled. "Ready for the real thing? If it looks this good on cheap paper, wait until you see it on the board."

I popped the top of the soda and let the orange fizz slide down my throat. "Let's do it," I said.

I SPENT ALL AFTERNOON CAREFULLY drawing a ti leaf lei all around the backside of Jay's surfboard. After thinking about it, I added another strand crossing the board diagonally across the center.

That's right.

Nili-boy brought me a burger and fries around two o'clock, but I ate so fast I barely tasted them. Nili-boy studied the board while I threw the rubbish away.

"I don't know how you do it," he said. "All the ti leaf ends pointing in like that—I bet from far away that lei looks j'like shark teeth in an open jaw. And with the second lei coming across—circle slash, yeah? J'like a big 'no bite' sign! Perfect!"

"Choice," proclaimed Rad when the last paint pen was put away and all the stray pieces of tape were in the trash. "Jay may have a career as a surfer, but guaranz you can have a career customizing boards. When the other surfers see that—watch out. Neither you nor Jay's gonna be able to blend into the background again."

"It's okay?" I asked. "Not too much? Not too ugly?"

Nili-boy gave me five. "Eh, if Jay won't surf again, I'll take his board!"

Rad laughed. "If Jay gives up surfing, there's no way I'm going to let you take this into the water. This board is going on a wall somewhere in Waikiki. This is art!"

I puffed a little at the praise.

Art! My art! On a wall in Waikiki!

I squinted at the board, trying to imagine it floating in the ocean against a bright white sky.

The cream background looks like underside of a turtle. Add dark shadows of arms and legs dangling over the sides like turtle fins—that's bad.

But then I remembered what Uncle Kahana said about Niuhi sharks. From far away, the light cream would make the lei stand out and the lei would look like open shark's jaws with the crossing line saying no, like a "no smoking" or "no crossing" or "no dogs allowed" sign.

No biting. No bite.

Up close, surfer close, you could see that the shark jaws and teeth were really a lei, a twisted ti leaf lei.

Intentional. It's all about manners. Please let it be enough to keep Jay safe. To make him feel safe.

"So, Leonardo, with a back like that, what're you going put on the front?" asked Rad.

I blinked. I hadn't considered the front. The underneath was what was important. "I dunno. A green stripe down the middle?" I said.

"Simple is good," said Rad. "How about two green stripes—the two main greens you used on the back separated by a thin black line going right down the middle?"

"Okay."

"Fantastic." He clapped his hands. "Can't freehand straight lines, even as good as you are, Zader. Now you'll get a chance to learn how to use the spray gun."

When the back was completely dry, we flipped it and started on the front. It took a lot longer than I thought it would to create three simple straight lines. Each line had to be masked and taped off and allowed to dry before the next line was added. I was starting to get antsy about the time. I needed to get back home before Mom-dem did from Waikiki. Nili-boy noticed my nervous jiggling.

"Eh, Zader, you gotta 5-4-4? Lua's just inside and to the right."

"I don't need to pee."

"What then? You're hopping like a bufo after a cricket."

"Late."

Nili-boy looked up from peeling the last piece of tape from the board and noticed for the first time how dark night had gotten outside our pool of light.

"Shoots!" he said.

Rad turned from the sink where he'd been fiddling with the spray gun. "I forgot. Stealth mission, right?"

I nodded, wondering how long I'd be grounded if Mom found out I'd lied about being sick and staying home.

Maybe free by my thirtieth birthday. Maybe.

"Nili, better help a braddah out and get Cinderella home

before he loses his glass slipper." He attached a different nozzle to the spray gun and shot some air through it. "I can shoot the final clear coat and let it dry while I work on other things."

Nili-boy nodded and gathered up the trash bag. "Sounds good. I'll take Z home and come back and help. You want something? I'm gonna feed Little Cuz before I drop him off. I can hear his opu rumbling from here. "

I looked at Nili-boy. "Nalani sometimes works the night shift at Hari's."

He threw his arm around my shoulder. "We can only hope, brah, hope!"

24
CHRISTMAS EVE HORROR STORY

~Kaona: a hidden or concealed meaning or reference to a person, place, or thing.~

"Nice, yeah?" Dad said.

"Yeah." Mom rocked lightly in her chair.

We were sitting on the front lanai after dinner. The sun was headed into the ocean, and the tradewinds carried a hint of rain down from the mountains. The Christmas tree lights were on in the house and the glow spilled out through the front windows. Lili was finishing the dishes in the kitchen and we could hear Jay in the bedroom lightly picking and strumming *Lahaina Days* on his 'ukulele.

I was sitting on the stairs, leaning against the banister, and doing a final light sanding on my gift for Lili. Trapped in the driftwood wasn't a dolphin or a whale, but a shark—a sleek and lean shark with a twist in his body as if turning to look behind him.

Over the last couple of weeks as I shaved him from his wooden prison, the gray wood revealed a rich, dark core, more like koa or ironwood than simple gray driftwood. The light and dark stippling in the grain gave him skin like a tiger shark, but not quite.

I stroked and sanded with a fine grit paper until I couldn't find a spot that wasn't beach glass smooth.

Time to oil.

Using an old sweat sock, I daubed a little orange oil on it, caressing along the grain to push the oil deep. Lili knew I was making her something, but she hadn't seen it yet.

"Eh, hui the house," called Uncle Kahana from the street. I could see him silhouetted against the sky, standing near the hibiscus hedge and holding something in his hands.

"Aloha, Uncle!" called Dad. "Come, come! Good to see you! Merry Christmas!"

Uncle Kahana started up the driveway, Ilima at his heels. "Mele Kalikimaka!" He jiggled the pan he was carrying. "Ilima and I brought you some kulolo. Figured I had too much for the luau tomorrow and I knew how much Liz likes it."

"Mahalo, Uncle Kahana." Dad rose from his chair to take it. "Want to come inside?"

"No, no," said Uncle Kahana. "It's too nice out." He handed Dad the foil-covered pan and sat down on the stairs across from me.

Ilima flopped down and rested her head on my foot. I reached out and patted her head. "Good girl," I cooed.

"You're sure you can spare it, Uncle?" Mom asked biting her lip. "You're cooking for a hundred, right?"

Startled, he glanced up at her. "Yeah," he said slowly, "but other people are bringing food, too. Cookies, rice pudding, apple strudel—things like that. Hawaiian food is the main menu, but everybody wants their favorites at Christmas."

"I'm amazed you stopped by," Mom said. "Cooking for such a crowd, I thought you wouldn't have time."

Ilima perked her ears and shivered.

"What do you mean, Liz? I already told you we're cooking all day tomorrow and eating early evening. This is just something I made small kine today. The big cooking happens tomorrow."

"Speaking of cooking, Uncle, you ate?" Dad interjected. "We just finished. Chicken stir-fry. Lots of leftovers. Easy to make you a plate."

"No, mahalo," said Uncle Kahana. He narrowed his eyes at Mom.

Mom inhaled to speak.

"How about a drink?" rushed Dad, careful to not look at Mom. "I'll take this kulolo back to the kitchen, slice it up, and come back with drinks."

"Sounds—" started Uncle Kahana.

"Shibai," said Mom.

Ilima ears drooped and she pressed harder on my foot.

"Shibai, shibai, shibai!" Mom declared. "Nobody will tell you, but nobody believes for one second that you're cooking dinner for a hundred people tomorrow."

Uncle Kahana leaned back against a post, eyes narrowed to daggers. He took a breath.

"I believe," I said.

Mom's laser beams turned to me. "What did you say?"

"I said I believe." I swallowed.

"You believe this old man's pupule story about cooking a Christmas luau on a private beach not on Oahu for one hundred friends we never met?" Mom stopped rocking and turned to me in her chair. "Fo'real?"

I sneaked a peek at Uncle Kahana. He was watching me very closely with an odd half-smile on his face. He gave me a faint nod. *Answer her*, he seemed to say.

I turned and faced Mom. "If Uncle Kahana says he's cooking for his friends on a private beach, then I believe him. He's never lied to me." I gave him small kine side-eye. "Even if I can't go to this place myself."

Uncle Kahana's smile grew until it shone from ear to ear. He reached out and patted my knee. "Bumbai, you'll come," he whispered. "Bumbai." He cleared his throat. "Yeah, Paul," he said to Dad. "A drink and some kulolo sounds maika'i, mahalo."

Mom stared at us for a long moment, then shook her head.

"Liz," said Dad, "it's Christmas. Come help me in the kitchen."

Mom slowly rose to her feet and took the kulolo from Dad. She lifted a corner of the foil and inhaled. "Smells 'ono, Uncle," she said gently. "Kulolo is my very favorite at Christmas. Mahalo." She turned to the screen door, opened it halfway, then turned back. "You like extra ice in your drinks, right?"

"Yeah, thanks, Liz," said Uncle Kahana.

Ilima chuffed.

"Oh, can you bring a bowl of ice water for Ilima?" he asked.

"Of course, of course," Mom said as she and Dad entered the house.

Uncle Kahana shifted his weight, regarding me in the fading light. "You really believe?" he asked.

I shrugged. "Yeah."

I either say I believe or call it shibai now and never have a chance to decide for myself. I want to know.

He watched me for another moment. I didn't even breathe.

He's not a mind-reader, right?

Finally, he nodded. "I think you do. Good. There's hope for you yet." Ilima licked my toes and I shivered. He gestured to the carving in my hands. "Let me see," he said.

I handed the shark to him and he held it up in the red and gold light of the Christmas tree. The sun finally dipped below the horizon and twilight ended, calling in the night.

"Shark," he said.

I nodded.

The yard lights flicked on, harsh, but not as harsh as the big overhead lanai lights would be. The yard lights were good. Enough light to see, but not enough to attract bugs.

"What shark?" Jay asked as he stepped through the doorway.

"This one," said Uncle Kahana.

"For Lili?" Jay asked.

I nodded. Jay stood there awkwardly, 'ukulele hanging by his side.

"Come. Sit," said Uncle Kahana. He flicked his eyebrows at Jay. "You gonna sing for us?"

"Ah, no. I was just fooling around." He reached beside one of the rockers and grabbed a metal folding chair leaning against the house. With a snap of his wrist and a kick of his foot, he opened it and sat.

"Keep fooling around," said Uncle Kahana. "You sound pretty good. Bumbai if you work hard you'll be really good."

Jay looked down at his feet and shrugged. Uncle Kahana turned the shark around in his hands, then held it out to Jay. "Like Z-boy over here. He has real talent. Look."

Jay sat his 'ukulele down on the table and reached for the shark. He looked at it, trailing a finger along its spine.

"Both of you have lots of talent. Shame if you waste 'em, yeah?" Uncle Kahana watched as Jay continued mapping the shark's shape with his finger, pausing at its closed mouth. "Now, Z-boy, what kind of shark is that?"

I looked up from petting Ilima's neck. "I dunno," I said.

Uncle Kahana tilted his head to the side, considering. "It blends, yeah? One line from a tiger shark, another from a great white, and one from a mako, I think." He squinted, then pointed. "One thing's certain; it's a shark."

"Yeah," Jay agreed.

"Niuhi shark?" asked Uncle Kahana shooting a bolt of lightning down my spine.

"No," I blurted. "No! It's for Lili—" I paused, confused.

"What?" Jay asked. "What's a Niuhi shark?"

Uncle Kahana smiled and reached for the carving. "No, Z-boy, you're right. Whatever kind of shark this is, it's not Niuhi." He took the tail gently between his thumb and fingers and stroked along the grain. "It doesn't feel Niuhi."

Jay looked from me to Uncle Kahana and back again. "What's Niuhi?"

Uncle Kahana stopped petting the shark and handed it back to me. He turned to look at Jay directly. "Niuhi sharks, J-boy," he said, "are man-eaters. No matter what you heard, only one kind of shark hunts and eats man and that's Niuhi."

Jay sat back in his chair and scoffed. "You're behind the times, Uncle Kahana. Plenny sharks bite people: bull shark, great white, tiger, hammerhead—"

"No. Only one kind: Niuhi."

"No, I saw it on Shark Week! In Australia—"

"You surf Australia?"

Jay blinked. "No," he said.

"Then why are you worried about Australian sharks?"

"I'm not, I—"

"Good. Then listen to your uncle. In Hawaii nei there's only one kind of shark to worry about: Niuhi."

"Niuhi?" Jay looked around the lanai. "What kind is that?"

"Told you," said Uncle Kahana. "Man-eater." He smiled. "Or man-biter. Depends on the mood."

"What!" Jay gulped.

Ilima raised her head off my foot and barked. "Kulikuli, Ilima," chastened Uncle Kahana. "I'm getting to it." He motioned her to lie back down.

"Everything okay out there?" called Mom from the kitchen.

"Yeah," I hollered. "Uncle Kahana's just telling us about sharks."

Lili bumped open the screen door with her hip, her hands busy with a tray loaded with a pitcher, tall iced glasses, and a bowl. I slipped my shark behind my back and covered it with the orange oil rag.

"Sharks?" she said, "Get choke hula about sharks." She set the tray down on the table and picked up the bowl. "Here, Ilima, for you," she called as she set it on the lanai. Ilima padded over, sniffed her feet, then lapped a drink. Lili lifted a glass from the tray. She pivoted gracefully, holding it out. "For you, Uncle. Lemonade?"

"Shoots," he said, taking the glass. He tipped it towards her. "Mahalo, Lili."

Lili said, "The boys in my halau are learning a new shark hula. It's about these guys in a canoe who are lost in the ocean. A shark comes and leads them back to land." She sidestepped, then 'uwehe'd, arms out. "Real powerful."

Uncle Kahana sipped the lemonade. "'Ono, Lili. Cold and little bit sour, little bit sweet. Perfect." He smacked his lips. "Plenny hula and oli honor sharks. Sharks have helped our people for a long, long time. Guided us, protected us—"

"Protected us?" Jay squeaked. "You just said sharks eat humans!"

Lili flopped down on the porch swing. Ilima jumped up and laid her head in Lili's lap, abandoning me.

Lili glared at Jay over the rim, the glass halfway to her mouth. "And what do you know? You ever listen to my kumu hula talk about sharks?" She sniffed and took a drink. "Too many Shark Week shows."

I looked at Jay with his knees bent and feet on the seat, arms wrapping it all.

Nothing dangling.

I cleared my throat. "Uncle, you were telling us about Niuhi sharks."

"Ah, Niuhi sharks." He settled a little more deeply on the stairs, resting his glass on his knee.

"What do they look like?" Jay asked.

"Good question, J-boy, but hard to answer. They can look anykine." He motioned with his hands. "Big, medium, super ginormous, even small. The older the shark, the bigger." He shrugged, jiggling the ice in his glass. "But it's not the size, it's the intent. It's what's in the heart of a shark that make it Niuhi or not."

"Bubbles," Jay said. "All your talk is bubbles! Heart?" Jay blew a puff of air. "Sharks don't have heart! Instincts, Uncle, only instincts. Everyone knows sharks hunt humans because they're easy pickings."

Uncle Kahana shook his head. "Bulai," he said. "Sharks hunt people? Bulai. If that were true, Jay, the water would be red from here to Pu'uwai to Kailua-Kona."

Truth. If we tasted like ice cream nobody could surf.

Uncle Kahana pressed his lips and wrinkled his nose.

"Most sharks, they're just like a bull in his pasture, minding his own beeswax, thinking his bully thoughts, wondering what the wahine cows are up to. If you enter the pasture quietly, with respect, he's gonna ignore you. You can pick mangoes, whatever. No biggie. If he doesn't want you there he'll snort a little, maybe paw the ground—that's when you know to leave." Uncle Kahana waved away a moth. "But take that same bull and jump in the pasture yelling and waving a red cape, and guaranz that bugger will stomp you into guava jelly." He took a sip. " Same with sharks. That's all the Shark Week shows, waving flags at bulls."

"They show what sharks can do," Jay said.

Uncle Kahana snorted. "If you chum the water, keep bloody fish near your body, swim in murky water or at night or where the river meets the ocean—in other words, if you act like prey, then don't be surprised if you end up missing a limb."

Jay flinched and hugged his knees tightly.

Uncle Kahana took another sip. "Respect, yeah? Just like you respect the bull's pasture, his home, you don't go into the ocean acting like prey. You ever notice almost every time someone gets bit by a shark it's a tourist? They don't know our ocean and our ocean doesn't know them. Respect, both sides."

"Respect?" scoffed Jay. "For what? You're still talking bubbles, Uncle Kahana."

Uncle Kahana weighed his words carefully. "Jay," he said, "you're in a really hard place right now. You've been filling your head with shark facts and stories that don't matter. Listen to your uncle. Sharks are not your enemy. They're not out to get you. Niuhi are the only sharks you need to worry about in these waters and there are ways to keep yourself safe."

"How do you know?"

"How do I know?"

"Yeah. How you know?" demanded Jay, his chin resting on his knees.

"How do I know what?" Uncle Kahana snagged a piece of ice with his teeth. "How to be safe or about Niuhi?"

"Niuhi."

Uncle Kahana crunched the ice, thinking. "Niuhi shark. Once you've seen a Niuhi shark, you know the difference. Other sharks are just Ferdinands in the pasture."

"You've seen one?" Jay asked.

Here it comes.

Uncle Kahana brushed his arm. "I was very young the first time I saw a Niuhi shark. There were these guys from Kailua, I think, who wanted to go fishing at Keikikai with a big hukilau net. You kids know what I'm talking about? Hukilau—where they put a huge net into the ocean and the whole community stands on the beach pulling it in?"

We nodded. Lili started humming the song and making the hand motions.

"Yes, Lili, like that. My father, Bobby Nickels they used to call him—"

"Why?" I asked.

"Later," Uncle Kahana said. "That's another story. My father was a fisherman on the weekdays and worked as a hapa-haole musician on the weekends. See, Jay," he said, shaking a finger, "that's why I know you have 'ukulele talent." He swirled his ice, then drained the glass.

"Bobby Nickels found out about these guys from Kailua. He went down to the docks to talk with them. 'You can't use hukilau nets around here,' he said. 'Why?' they asked. 'Kapu!' he told them. 'It's forbidden to use big nets; you can only fish using small throwing nets or fishing line.'"

Uncle Kahana paused, holding out his glass. "A little more, Jay." Jay stood up and filled his glass, the lemonade melting the ice as it ran down the side. "Mahalo, J-boy," he said and took another sip.

He looked off into the distance. "Obeying kapu is important," he continued, "but back then people already didn't understand, didn't believe. 'You're crazy to believe that kine,' they said. 'Get plenny fish at Keikikai. We're pulling hukilau tomorrow. Come! Bring your family. Plenny kaukau for everybody.'

"Early the next morning, my father woke me up. He made two ti leaf leis and tied one around my ankle and put the other around his own. We went to the docks and took out the toro, riding the sail past the lava flow to Piko Point. When we got to Keikikai they were already dropping the net. 'Don't do this,' Daddy begged. 'This is a kids' beach! Think about our keiki in the water! Niuhi sharks live here. You're going to make them angry by breaking kapu! Hukilau nets take everything: good fish, trash fish, anykine!' But they never listened." Uncle Kahana closed his eyes and pinched the bridge of his nose.

"I remember there were a few guys working the net in the water. The day was calm, typical Keikikai. Clear. The sand bottom was only twenty feet or so. Suddenly, the hair raised on my arms. In the boat, I could feel chicken skin pop out all over my body and crawl up my spine and stick in my throat. 'Daddy,' I asked, 'what's that?' 'Kulikuli,' he told me. 'Too late. He stay come.'

"The first guy never made a sound. Just gone. Not even a manini ghost of red in the ocean. Nothing. 'Eh, where's Moki?' somebody asked. They could feel it too, but no one said what they already knew. Then one guy just treading water and holding onto the top of the net jerked once, like someone was pulling his leg. But then no more leg, then no more two legs, snip, like scissors, so fast, and blood blossomed in the water like red lehua in the mountains. That's when the screaming started."

Ilima whined and tucked a paw over her nose. Uncle Kahana smiled faintly at her, then looked at us, one by one. "A Niuhi shark was in the water and he was more than huhu over the net; he was rabid with anger. After the second bite, my father pulled me away from the side of the toro and took the sail down. 'Don't look,' Daddy said.

"I covered my ears and closed my eyes, but I remember lots of shrieking and splashing and then, worse, silence. Five guys got bit that day and three died; two bled out before they could get back to the beach, and the first guy, well, they never found anything. On the shore our friends and neighbors yelled 'shark' and 'get out of the water,' but I stayed in the middle of the toro holding my ears and squeezing my eyes—until the boat shifted hard to the right and water splashed on my skin. I opened my eyes, scared the shark bumped the boat, but it was my father. He jumped over the side and into the water."

Jay gasped. "Tutu Kane Kaulupali jumped in?"

"To save the guys, right?" Lili asked.

"No," I said slowly, "not to save them. They never listened. They deserved it. He jumped in the water for something else."

Uncle Kahana met my eyes, telling me something I didn't understand.

It wasn't the shark's fault, right?

"Why?" Lili asked. "Why did he jump?"

"The shark," said Uncle Kahana, finally blinking. "It was tangled in the net." He stared into the bottom of his glass, seeing what we couldn't imagine. "Daddy knew the shark would drown and die if it wasn't cut free. He jumped into the lehua water with his long boning knife, grabbing the net through the bloody blossoms and sawing away. I leaned over the side and looked down into the water. Daddy was so small and the shark so big! But he kept working, sliding his knife, slicing through the net. When Daddy got to the last loop trapping his tail, the shark turned, and Daddy's knife slipped, nicking the tip of the shark's tail. I thought this is it. Daddy'd freed the shark so it could feed on him. But the shark turned and paused. It looked Daddy in the eye, with that fierce, cold, jet black Niuhi mano eye. Bits of flesh and blood in the water between them, they stared at each other. But then Daddy had to take a breath. I watched

as he slowly rose to the surface, no faster than his bubbles, barely kicking."

Uncle Kahana shivered in the warm night. "I saw that Niuhi eye just once more. It looked into my young eyes peering over the edge of the boat, and I saw its Niuhi heart. I don't know what it saw in mine." He ran a hand through his hair, then rubbed his chin against his shoulder.

Uncle Kahana rolled his neck and shoulders, trying to ease the tension. He sighed. "Daddy broke the surface, took a breath, then looked back down. The Niuhi shark was circling under the toro, moving in and out of the blood red clouds like a car coming in and out of the fog. The other guys were already in their boats, motors roaring for the docks. Before it disappeared, I saw the Niuhi shark nudge what was left of the net on the sandy bottom. The next thing I remember is standing on Keikikai shore, watching the pink foam roll in, waiting for my Daddy to come back. He'd stayed out in the water to pick up all the bits of netting from the ocean floor he could find."

"After the shark attacks?" Jay breathed.

Uncle Kahana nodded.

"Why?"

Uncle Kahana looked up from his memories, surprised. "To keep the kids safe, of course."

"From what?" Mom asked stepping onto the lanai. In her hands was a plate of kulolo sliced into neat squares. Dad followed, closing the door behind them.

"Sharks," Lili said.

"Niuhi sharks," said Uncle Kahana.

"Uncle, you're not telling the kids about Tutu Kane Kau-lupali and the shark attacks are you?" Mom frowned. "That was a long time ago." She tipped her head at Jay behind his back, making sly-eye at Uncle Kahana. "No reason to bring up ancient history."

"Liz, you remember my father, Bobby Nickels?"

Mom snitched a piece of kulolo and a drink, then sat in her rocker. She kicked back, rocking slightly. "Yes," she said, "I remember. He was a big Hawaiian man. Hard to believe he's related to you!"

Uncle Kahana chuckled. "Remember what he used to tell you keikis every time he heard you were headed to the beach?"

"He'd call to my mother, 'Elizabeth Kamaile! Lei, don't forget your lei!' I remember him chasing my mother down the beach, waving a ti leaf at her. 'Put a lei on that keiki! I taught you better than this!'" Mom smiled. "Ho, how mad my mother would get because of him! He kept telling her, 'Mind your manners! Have respect!'"

"Why was she mad?" Lili asked.

"Because she wanted to be modern. She didn't want to drag all those ancient superstitions around. She didn't want to make 'A' in front of her friends."

"But you wore a lei at the beach," said Uncle Kahana. "Your brother, James, too."

"My Dad used to wear leis in the ocean?" asked Lili.

Mom smiled. "I forgot that. He used to wear one surfing, a twisted ti leaf lei, I think. Just here, around his ankle. Plenny kids used to wear 'em like that."

"I still wear a ti leaf lei every time I go in the water," said Uncle Kahana.

"Fo'real?" Mom asked.

"Guaranz. I won't bring pork over the pali at night, I won't whistle during a full moon, and I won't 'au'au in the ocean without a ti leaf lei."

Mom shook her head and sipped her drink.

"Easier than arguing, I imagine." Dad crossed to his rocker and sat down. "Considering how flexible all you Kaulupalis are."

I laughed, then caught Mom's eye and quit.

I guess some things are funny when they're true.

"It's not about the ti leaf, not really," said Uncle Kahana. "It's what the lei represents. Respect. Manners. It reminds everybody how to behave. It helps us recognize each other. I keep thinking about how that Niuhi shark turned to look at my father j'like he wanted to make sure who he was. Like he was memorizing his face, yeah? But in that shark's turn away from him, that was grace. The shark could've killed us all, but he chose not to. It's like the line in your carving, Zader. That's what it reminded me of."

"What carving?" asked Lili.

Uncle Kahana's eyes popped wide. "Nothing, nothing," he said. "Forget that part."

"What part? What're you guys talking about?" Lili wheedled.

"More lemonade?" asked Jay giving me side-eye as he jumped up and held out the pitcher to Lili.

She gave him a funny-kine smile knowing something

was up, but letting it pass. "No, thank you," she said. "But I'll take a piece of kulolo." Jay handed her one. She took a bite. "Ummm, 'ono, Uncle." With her other hand she patted Ilima's head. "Good girl," she said. Ilima chuffed and rolled over so Lili could scratch her belly.

"Uncle?" said Jay, waving the pitcher.

"No. Get plenny, mahalo."

Jay set the pitcher back on the table and sat on his chair. He rocked back on two legs, swaying.

"J-boy, a few weeks ago you saw a shark off Nalupuki."

Jay shrugged and looked away.

"Yeah," said Uncle Kahana gently, "you did. Don't lie now. Tell me about the shark."

Lili and I held our breaths. Even Ilima was still, waiting. Mom and Dad exchanged *did-you-know?-no-did-you?-no* glances. "Shark Week," mouthed Mom. Dad nodded. *That explains it*, his eyes said.

Jay wouldn't look at us; he kept his eyes on a corner of the lanai where a gecko stood in the shadows doing push-ups.

Finally, softly, he spoke.

25
Jay's Shark Tale

~A'o: to learn, coach, teach, advise, prescribe.~

"The waves were junk," Jay started. "I was just drifting on my board. Frankie was paddling out. The light was bright. I could see the bottom, forty, fifty feet down. The day was warm, but then all of a sudden I got chicken skin. I don't know why; I wasn't cold, the wind wasn't blowing. I rubbed my arms and looked down in the water. That's when I saw it."

"Saw what?" asked Lili.

"The bullet shape. It was huge. Bigger a whale, I think."

"What? No way! Cannot," Lili scoffed.

Jay turned to her. "Can," he said. "Was. No joke. No shibai. It cruised in from deep water and was headed toward Piko Point."

"Jay," said Uncle Kahana, "was that when you yelled 'shark' and came flying in like Jaws was on your 'okole?"

"No," said Jay. "I was shocked. My chicken skin had chicken skin, but I wasn't freaked out until it –"

"Until it what?" I asked.

Jay turned to me. "Behind it was another shark, like a

baby compared to the first one even though sharks don't raise their babies. That little one swam out from behind the big shark and came closer, maybe thirty feet away, looked me right in the eye, and grinned."

Lili and I leaned back, stunned.

"I know, I know, I sound pupule, but I swear that little shark *grinned* showing me all its teeth! And I was more afraid of the little one than the big one. That's when I yelled 'shark' and hele'd on out of the water."

"Jay, this is important now," said Uncle Kahana. "Were any of the sharks missing the tip of its tail fin?"

"No." Jay paused. "The big one, I didn't notice the tail. It all happened too fast. The little one wasn't missing anything. The tail was whole, I think."

"Wait," said Lili. "You had chicken skin because something was warning you, right? Just like the warning Uncle got in the boat."

"Yeah, maybe," Jay said.

"But when you saw a monster shark, you weren't scared. You only panicked after seeing the small one." Lili shook her head. "Jay, I've seen plenny small-kine reef sharks. I know you have, too. I heard you and Frankie talking about all the little black tip reef sharks and baby hammerheads out there. Why did the little one scare you? It doesn't make sense."

"Makes perfect sense," said Uncle Kahana. "I told you, big, small—it doesn't matter. Even the tiniest shark bite in the right place can kill a human faster than he can get to shore. That's what Jay recognized. Not the size, but the nature. Niuhi. A shark that knows, that chooses."

We sat there on the lanai, letting Uncle Kahana's words wash over us. I had heard this before, but it was new to Jay and Lili. I watched the emotions roll over Jay's face as he thought about it. "Niuhi chooses," he repeated.

Uncle Kahana nodded. "Niuhi are very, very rare. They live a long, long time. In Hawaii nei, Niuhi sharks can guide us to land when we're lost or bite us 'til we bleed out. Most of the time they ignore us; that's why shark attacks aren't common here. But once in a while you can draw their attention—and that can be a bad thing."

"The small one was Niuhi," said Jay.

"Yes," said Uncle Kahana. "Probably the big one, too."

"I got its attention."

"Yes, Jay, you did. And then instead of acting with respect, you acted like prey. It was young. You're lucky it didn't chase you and bite you for fun."

"What did the shark do when you panicked?" asked Lili.

Jay picked at a fingernail. "Nothing. Swam back to the big one. They kept heading out to the point."

"Jay," said Dad, "why didn't you tell us before?"

Jay shrugged. "What's the point? You can't do anything if I'm the one sitting out there on a surfboard, legs and arms dangling like bait."

"Jay, you can't stay out of the water forever," said Dad. "We live on an island. You love the ocean. You need it like—"

"Air," Mom interrupted.

Uncle Kahana crossed his arms. "Now J-boy, the sharks never rushed you?"

"No."

"Never circled you?"

"No."

"Never bumped your board?"

"No. I got out of the water too fast."

Uncle Kahana snorted. "Yeah, keep telling yourself that, J-boy. If a Niuhi shark wanted you—"

"He'd have you," I said. "But all he did was grin?"

"Yeah," said Uncle Kahana. "And how you know that wasn't a howzit grin?"

"A howzit grin?" Jay made a face.

"You mean like when somebody beeps their horn and flashes shaka?" Lili laughed.

Uncle Kahana smiled. "Maybe that's the way Niuhi sharks make shaka!"

"James Kapono, look at me," Mom said in her no-questions voice. "Uncle Kahana is right. Your ancestors knew it. My Tutu Kane who swam with a Niuhi shark without fear knew it. It's all about respect. Wear a ti leaf lei and get back in the ocean. Pau already. Now pass me the kulolo and let's talk about what Santa could be bringing!"

26
One Shark, No Bite

~Shaka: a hello or howzit hand gesture made with thumb and pinkie extended,
other fingers folded.~

The day after Christmas I was sitting on a bench at the
pavilion above Keikikai and Nalupuki beaches watching Jay show off his new paint job.

"Ho," said Frankie, "from here it looks j'like shark jaws!
But when you're close you realize it's a lei."

"That's your old board, Jay?" asked Char Siu.

"Yeah. Zader did the custom paint and Lili got me the
new leash for Christmas."

"Wow! Zader did this?" Char Siu ran her finger along
the edge.

"Nili-boy and Rad helped," I said.

"Rad? The old haole guy from Lauele Surf?" Frankie
asked.

"Yeah. They filled the dings and shot the clear coat."

"But the art's yours," said Char Siu. "Sharp."

Frankie touched the front of the board. "Waxed and
ready. New leash, new board, let's go try 'em out."

I glanced toward Nalupuki. The sky was dark along the

far horizon and the wind was picking up. The waves were a little sloppy, but not very big. A small storm was blowing out at sea, not yet ready to come to shore. The Keikikai side was mostly empty, just a few scattered families with kids trying out Christmas boogie boards and new flashing fins.

Jay lifted his board and shifted his weight, looking out toward Piko Point. He fingered the leash, his thoughts far away.

"Eh," said Frankie, bumping his arm. "We're going or what?"

"In a minute," said Jay. "I need to talk with Zader first."

"Shoots," said Frankie. "See you out there. Laters, Zader, Char Siu." He balanced his board under an arm and headed down to the beach.

"You gonna fly Iolani?" Char Siu asked me. My stunt kite was resting on the table waiting for the moment he could stretch his wings.

"In a minute, Char Siu."

Char Siu looked at me and Jay, then smiled. "I'll be over by the showers. Call when you're ready."

"'Kay," I said, but she was already walking away.

"You sure you want stand out on the hillside?" Jay asked. "Might rain."

I looked at the sky and the gathering storm, considering. "I have a jacket and umbrella and shoes on. Should be okay."

"But what if it's not?"

I shrugged. "Can't stay under the pavilion forever," I said.

Jay stood his board on end, the underside toward us. He reached out and traced part of the lei. "I know what you and Uncle Kahana are trying to do."

"What?" I asked like shave ice wouldn't melt in my mouth.

Jay gave me side-eye. "You want me to believe in a fairy tale."

I stood and swung my arms, loosening the joints. "Maybe it doesn't matter what you believe," I said. I gestured toward Piko Point where the surfers were lined up. "Maybe it's more about what they believe."

"Niuhi."

I shrugged. "If it's the lei and not the ti leaf, and if the shark chooses like Uncle Kahana claims, then your board says it all."

"Respect? Manners?" he scoffed.

"Maybe," I said.

"If not?"

I shrugged again, looking at the sky. "Can't stay hidden inside forever." I picked up Iolani and my umbrella from the table and headed toward the showers, eyes on the hill where Iolani could soar.

KAHANA WAS SITTING NEXT TO Pohaku at Piko Point watching the surfers. "Oh, the food was so 'ono, Pohaku" he said, "The kalua pig was falling off the bone and just the right amount of salty. Made the poi taste extra sweet." He sighed.

Kahana relaxed and let Pohaku fill his mind.

Warmth held from the sun. Contentment. Pleasure at Kahana's happiness and company. Slowly, a question rose to the surface of Kahana's mind like a bubble from the ocean floor: *But where is thy companion?*

"You won't believe it, Pohaku. Ilima's at home, recuperating." He chuckled. "Last night after the party Vicki offered to fly Ilima home because the year before Don stumbled on the landing and almost dumped her off. I teased Ilima that it was because she ate too much Mexican food that night. She loves it even though the beans give her pilau gas fo'days! Ilima's kind of sensitive about her weight and didn't believe it was a joke. Besides, I'm always telling her to lay off the cookies, right?

"Anyway, yesterday morning the whole crew flew in because we had a ton of stuff for the party. Nick thought it would be easier to fill the cutter than to load everybody up like pack mules. But coming back there was only the two of us, so Vicki and Rudy offered to fly us home.

"Imagine: Ilima's holding on to Vicki, and we're coming into Keikikai. Just as we hit the sand, Vicki fake stumbles, just playing, but Ilima's so nervous she jumped right off and tumbled, roll, roll, rolling! You should have seen her! Sand everywhere, up her nose, in her ears, her teeth, and when she finally stands up, there's a crab holding on to her tail." Uncle Kahana shook his head. "We couldn't help it; it was hilarious! Rudy, Vicki, and I almost peed our pants!" He wiped an eye. "But you know Ilima; her nose is out of a joint a little bit right now. She says she's on a diet and needs to rest after the party." Kahana snorted. "Chee, only Ilima needs for rest up after a day at Respite Beach!"

More bubbles rising from the ocean floor, laughter and chagrin for Ilima's sake. Then another question: *The boy?*

"Ah, yes, the boy," said Kahana. He stood and looked out to the surfers' line up. "There's Jay," he pointed.

W ITH ONE LAST PUSH, JAY crested the wave, the wind blowing spray back into his face. He flicked his hair back and paddled on, coming to rest at the end of the surfers' line. "What's up, Frankie," he said.

"Jay! Howzit!" said Frankie. He pointed with his chin. "Look. Nili-boy's behind you."

Coming through the last break before the swells smoothed out, Nili-boy raised a hand, flashing shaka. He cruised over the top of the last roller and headed toward them.

Frankie, eyeing the first wave of a new set, turned toward the shore, and starting paddling into position. "This one's mine," he called. "Weeehaa!"

Jay slid down the backside as the face of the wave formed and lifted Frankie. Effortlessly and as smooth as haupia on a lazy afternoon, Frankie coasted all the way to the sand. Beached, he got out of the water, fiddling with his leash. Two other surfers in line took the next good waves, leaving Jay and Nili-boy bobbing on their boards, waiting for the next set.

"Good to see you out here, Cuz," said Nili-boy.

Jay ran a hand along the edge of his board. "Thanks, Nili-boy, for helping Zader with my board."

Nili-boy puffed up his cheeks and blew the air out, tossing his head back and flinging his dripping bangs off his face. "Was nothing," he said. "The board's finish is smooth, but Zader's art makes it. He's the one with the talent."

"Yeah."

"You, too, Little Cuz. Don't give up."

"Nili—" he began.

Jay felt it. It started as a low hum that buzzed around in his blood and raised the hair on his arms. He whipped his head around. No waves and a long, long, long stroke to the beach.

"Yeah, Jay, I feel 'em, too," whispered Nili-boy. "Niuhi."

Jay turned to Nili-boy and followed his eyes out past Piko Point. Jutting from the water, first the tip of one sleek black triangle, now two, the second much much larger than the first. Keeping his eyes on the fins, Nili-boy said "You see 'em?"

"Yeah."

"Two, one big, one smaller."

"Yeah."

"You wearing your lei?"

"No."

Nili-boy swallowed. "Good thing you have that board then." He cut his eyes at Jay. Jay was pale, but holding it together. "Breathe, braddah, breathe! Slow. Remember, Jay, calm. Don't panic. The Niuhi are way over there. Don't wave any red flags."

Jay nodded, but that buzzing buzzing like soda fizzing, buzzing in his brain that kept telling him to run, to flee, to act like—

"Prey," he said.

"Shoots, brah, I already praying," said Nili-boy.

The two sets of fins sliced the water along the edge of Piko Point where Jay saw Uncle Kahana standing next to Pohaku, a hand shading his eyes from the glare. Uncle Kahana was watching, keeping his body in line with the fins, pointing as they slid by. The sharks strolled near the very end of the point where deep water met the reef. A pause, then the smaller one parted ways with the big one, turning toward shore and Jay and Nili-boy. Its dorsal fin slipped below the surface.

Buzzing, buzzing. Then silence. "If it wants to bite us there's nothing we can do," whispered Jay.

"Never was, Cuz," said Nili-boy. "In the ocean or on the shore, don't forget ohana is family and family is who you and they say it is."

"Niuhi?"

"Yeah."

"*Family?*"

"Always," said Nili-boy.

The storm was creeping inland and the sky was

overcast; the water reflected the clouds, keeping its secrets down close in the shadows. Out of the corner of his eye, Jay caught movement. A sleek bullet shape, small and deadly, regarded him from below. It rolled its body away from him as it cruised past, its eye cold and fierce as the Niuhi shark examined both the drawing on the board and the boy riding it. Passing once, twice, it flashed its teeth at Jay. With a flick of its tail, it headed out to sea.

A minute later they saw the smaller fin break the surface near the larger fin lounging off Piko Point. With a final swish of tail fins, both sharks dipped below the surface disappearing into the deep dark water.

Jay breathed a sigh of relief. "One shark,—one Niuhi shark—no bite."

Nili-boy heard his sigh and laughed, splashing water at him. "I think she likes you," he said.

"What?"

"Sure. I saw the way she looked at you."

"She?"

"The little Niuhi shark. It was a female, young. What, did you think she was coming over to eat you?" Nili-boy teased. "She was checking you out! You saw teeth flash? That's shaka shark-style."

"Why?"

Nili-boy laughed some more. "Like I know why wahines do anykine. Chillax, Jay. Let's ride some waves." Nili-boy turned his board, paddling and kicking to catch the next wave.

Bobbing on his board alone in the ocean, Jay watched

Nili-boy take off. He leaned down, pulled his legs on his board, and paddled to the sweet spot where the next good wave would carry him to shore. He paused for a moment, caressing the backside of his board for luck.

Well, at least this lei can't fall off, he thought.

27
HIGH NOON

~Pau: finished; completed; through.~

I didn't want to be home, I didn't want to be training at Uncle Kahana's with Char Siu and Jay, and I didn't want to be out on the reef at Piko Point with no protection, but that's where I was headed. I ignored the burning saltwater splashing over the edges of my slippahs as I dashed across the rocks, run, run, running away.

Any place but where I am. Anyone but me.

At the very edge of the lava flow, I had to stop. Surrounded by water, I swallowed pain in gasping gulps. This pain was different, a hard ball deep in my guts that dwarfed the blisters on my feet.

Jump in, I thought. *Let go.*

In some ways it would be a relief.

The letter came today, the letter that said 'thank you for your application, but the number of qualified applicants had exceeded enrollment capacity—blah-blah-blah.'

I wasn't getting in. The decision was pau. I wasn't going to Ridgemont next year with Jay and Char Siu.

"I'm not going either," yelled Jay when Mom told us the news.

"Jay—" Mom said.

"No! It's a stupid school! If they don't want both of us, their loss! I'm not going!"

"Jay, we can talk about this later," Dad said.

"No! You don't understand! Zader needs me! He can't go to Lauele Intermediate alone!"

I stood in the kitchen, eye wide but unseeing.

Jay is throwing everything away because of me. He thinks I can't handle it on my own.

I fled out the back door, grabbed my slippahs, and started running until there was nowhere left to run.

Chest heaving with unshed tears, I walked to the edge of the big saltwater pool near Pohaku.

Just jump.

"Eh, panty," said a voice behind me.

I turned to face Alika. He was carrying a fishing pole, an empty bait bucket, and a smirk. His eyes lit up. "You crying?"

"Shut up, Alika. Go away."

He looked around the reef. "You're out here all alone, no Jay, no space suit? Wow, I didn't know it was my birthday."

"Just leave me alone. Go torture somebody else."

He grinned even wider. "You heard about Tuna? She got into Ridgemont. Got the letter today. Stupid tita thinks she's all that with a side of kimchee. But you, you out here alone crying your panty eyes out, I think you got a letter today, too."

"Shut up."

He stepped closer. I could see the stains on his shirt from breakfast—ketchup and bacon grease—and smelled the stale eggs on his breath. "Lauele Intermediate, brah. Me and you."

I glanced right and left, knowing what was there before I even looked—a wall of water all around. Nowhere to run.

"Every day." Alika inched closer. He reached out to push me. I didn't think. The lua 'ai flowed from my brain to my heart to my fist. I countered his push and used his momentum to bring my knee straight to his family jewels.

Primary target.

I missed.

"You bugger!" he yelled when my knee crashed into his thigh. "You like beef? Eat this!"

His fist popped my eye, and I stumbled backward, biting my lip as I landed on my side next to Pohaku. Little pockets of saltwater exploded, splashing my arm and leg, burning like acid, like snake venom, like Pele's own fire, lava roaring up and down my spine. I heard someone scream, the sound soaring past hearing and realized it was me.

"Freak!"

I looked up and saw Alika's face backlit by the noonday sun. Satisfied, he turned away.

Not worth his time.

The skin on my arm and leg was puckering, blistering, and turning gray; I could hear it crackle and hiss as I sat up.

Breathe, remember to breathe.

My breath caught once, twice in my throat, and then I

felt a switch flip deep inside. Instead of crushing me, the pain felt good; it tingled, sending energy snapping along my blistered limbs, moving the adrenaline from flight to something new and far more deadly. My senses were roaring; not only could I smell Alika's breakfast, I could also detect the lotion his grandmother used and see her handprint where she'd touched the back of his neck. My stomach rumbled as thoughts flickered faster than I could follow, narrowing like a laser to a single stark point: adapt or die.

Adapt or die? What does that even mean?

Like lightning, suddenly I *knew*. It was all so clear, like wandering out of the fog into the sunlight. I could deny these savage feelings building within me and continue to run and hide from the Alikas of the world, keeping my head and eyes down forever, or I could embrace the surge of strength that was rushing through me and raise my head high.

Surrounded by a wall of water, my senses heightened, my body strengthened, and my mind sharper than a surgeon's blade, I chose.

I'm tired of running. I'm tired of relying on Jay.

I raised myself off the reef ignoring the saltwater puddled around my feet and gathered my balance. My eyes narrowed against the bright light, and I started to move to the left, circling.

"Alika," I called softly. I felt the shark tooth necklace heavy against my chest.

Pumped with victory, he didn't even look at me as he fiddled with the line on his fishing pole. Caught up in his own power trip, he didn't even realize that I'd stood with no intention of running.

"Freak!" he snarled, wrapping the last bit of line and tucking the hook. "You want more?"

"Alika," I whispered, still circling, moving closer as I slid past his spine, curving along his shoulder.

It startled him when I suddenly appeared at his side. He lifted his head. His eyes met mine. With a bang and a wobble, the bucket and pole clattered against the reef, forgotten.

The vision in my right eye blurred. I shook my head to clear it. I licked my lip where I'd bit it and tasted blood, salty and sweet and oh, so 'ono I had to lick again. I grinned.

Alika paled, the cockiness gone. He stumbled a little, turning with me as I circled him like an eagle, a tiger, a *shark*. "You better leave me alone," he said.

"Alika," I purred, "you better run."

28
The Hero Returns

~I mua: to progress; to go forward; to claim to be senior, more than before.~

"**P**ono," I called as I opened the door. Jay and Char Siu were stretching on the lauhala mats, holding the pose while Uncle Kahana counted. Ilima rushed to me from her pillow, beating her tail against my legs as she hula'd hello. "Who's a little sweetheart, huh? Who? Yes, it's you, Ilima!" I knelt on a mat and ruffled her ears.

"Good grief, Z-boy, what happened to you?"

"Zader!" Char Siu said. "Your eye!"

"It's nothing."

"Nothing?" Jay exclaimed. He scrambled to his knees and reached toward my face, turning it gently as he examined the swelling around my eye, his fingers lightly brushing the cut on my lip. His mouth compressed into a thin, white line, his eyes fierce and remote. "Alika," he growled.

I nodded. "Out by Piko Point."

"I'm going to kill him," Jay said, leaping toward the door.

"There's no reason," I said. "It's pau."

"What?" Jay blinked, hand on the doorknob.

"Alika's not going to bother me again. He can't." I grinned so wide, my lip started to bleed again.

I had just enough time to see Jay's jaw drop when Uncle Kahana interrupted with a bag of ice wrapped in a dishtowel. "Everybody cool your jets. You can kill Alika later, Jay. We need to take care of Zader first. Come sit," he said, leading me to the stacked furniture. He lifted a kitchen chair, flipped it right-side up, and pushed me down. "Hold this." He put the towel in my hand and set it against my eye.

"Your arm!" Char Siu said.

I peeked at it with my good eye. "Yeah. I fell in some water," I chuckled, turning my ankle inward, showing off the side of my leg. "My leg, too."

"Hurts?"

"Not really. Itches li'bit."

"Zader." Uncle Kahana's concerned face swam into view. "Did you hit your head?"

Little sparks of light twinkled around Uncle Kahana, landing on his shoulders like Tinker Bell's dandruff. I wrinkled my nose, inhaling some of the sparks and recognizing the familiar fragrance of something close to sandalwood that I only smelled around Uncle Kahana. Ilima padded over and sat at my feet. I saw her sparkle, too.

Just add wings and tiara, I thought.

I snorted.

"Is he drunk?" Char Siu asked.

"Adrenaline and shock, I think. Zader, how many fingers?"

"Three."

Uncle Kahana flicked his wrist.

"Now two," I said. "I don't think I hit my head. Alika pushed me, I tried to go for his 'alas and missed, so he punched my eye and I fell into some saltwater and bit my lip. But that's the last time he's going to touch me. Ever."

Jay stood with his hand on the doorknob, unsure of what to do next. "Somebody saw him hit you and he's in trouble, right? He can't hurt you if he's locked up in Kailua Juvie where he belongs."

I shook my head no.

Jay closed his eyes, trying to wrap his head around it all. "His grandmother had enough of him and is finally sending him to his mother in Kona?"

"He's not going anywhere, Jay. Neither am I."

Ilima rose to delicately sniff my ankle and bloody knuckles before returning to my feet. She tilted her head at Uncle Kahana, exchanging a look I couldn't read.

He raised his eyebrows, then turned to me and spoke. "I see you cut your lip, Zader. But not all the blood on you is yours."

I looked down at my shirt and laughed. "Another shirt lost to Alika's bloody nose." At the looks on their faces I laughed again.

Whoa, my head feels a like a balloon floating two feet off my shoulders!

"What happened after Alika hit you, Zader?" Uncle Kahana squatted next to my chair and reached out to touch my leg. The warmth and strength of his hand steadied me; I felt all my drifting pieces start to pull back to center anchoring my head firmly to my neck.

I blinked a few times and cleared my throat.

Better.

"I told him I was done running. I told him from now on *he'd* better run."

"Just like that?" Char Siu asked.

"Yeah."

"An'den?" Jay asked.

"He ran. But I caught him."

"What you did you do to Alika, Zader?" I could feel Uncle Kahana holding his breath.

I rolled my head around my shoulders and slowly, gently, twisted from side to side. My spine popped in sharp staccato like a deck of cards in a dealer's hands. Deep inside my body I felt organs shifting and sliding, resettling themselves in ways that felt more normal. I was suddenly overwhelmingly tired.

I don't care if naps are for babies.

"Z-boy?" Uncle Kahana shook my leg.

I yawned.

"Stay with me, Zader. Where's Alika?"

I yawned again. "Home, I think. Unless I broke his nose like Jay did. I felt it crunch, just like whacking an egg against a bowl before you scramble it. Hey, you have any eggs, Uncle Kahana? I'm kinda hungry."

Uncle Kahana let his breath out in a giant rush and dropped his hand from my leg to Ilima's head. I felt sad I couldn't see the sparkles anymore. I liked them.

"You broke his nose?" Jay asked. He walked toward me, grim and worried.

"Awesome." Char Siu held out her knuckles for a bump.

Jay snorted. "I broke his nose and he still came after you. What makes you think he won't come after you again?"

"Because when *I* broke his nose, he didn't go to the office and call his grandma. He ran. Again. I chased him up the beach," I said. "I caught him near the showers at the pavilion. We had a little talk. I said if he thought I was going to be his personal punching bag at Lauele Intermediate, he was wrong. He said he was sorry and that he'd make sure Chad and the others left me alone. It's over."

"And you believed him?"

"No. I believed the pee running down his leg." I smirked.

Jay rocked his head back, then flopped on the floor mats. "No way."

"Way. It's pau." I looked down again at the front of my shirt. "After that, I didn't dare come close enough to touch him again, so I let him run home. Blood is bad enough."

Sometimes.

I poked at the sore spot on my lip with my tongue.

"Man, I wished I'd seen it."

I grinned, remembering. But I couldn't find the words to explain how I really knew it was over. Something fundamental had changed in me, and I knew in ways beyond blood and pee and pain that Alika recognized it, too. I'd seen it in his eyes and smelled it in his burnt metal stench, an oil slick of scent I tracked from the reef past the showers to the parking lot. It still lingered in the back of my throat.

I shifted in my chair, turning my good eye toward Jay. "All the way here I've been thinking. I want you to go to Ridgemont next year, Jay." I glanced at Char Siu. "Both of you."

He sobered and sat up. "I already told Mom and Dad I'm not going."

"Jay, they're right. You have to go. You can't throw this away."

"I'm not going without you."

"I don't want you to go without me either." I tried to laugh, but the sound was hollow and forced. "But if you're there you can coach me through the ninth grade applications. There's one more chance."

"So, we'll go together in ninth grade. I'll wait."

"Ninth grade is tougher. Fewer spots. I'm gonna need an inside man."

Jay shook his head, but I rolled past him. "Besides, are you really going to make Char Siu ride the bus next to Tunazilla?"

"Tuna got in?" Char Siu asked.

"Alika said."

"Lisa Ling's going, too." Jay was stubborn. "Char Siu can sit next to her."

I softened. "We can't always be together."

"I don't like it."

"You surf," I said.

"What has that got to do with anything?" Jay's eyes were confused, his mouth unhappy.

"I can't surf. You can't *not* surf. It's just how we are." I paused, taking the dishtowel away from my face. "You have to go to Ridgemont. It's your future. I'll be fine."

"You know, Z-boy, I think you will," said Uncle Kahana. "You want those eggs scrambled or sunny-side up?"

29
DREAM GIRL

~Niuhi: a man-eating shark that knows, that chooses.~

I knew when I went to sleep with my shark tooth necklace touching my skin I would dream. I hoped Dream Girl and I would go flying again, soaring over the red and orange fields, but this dream was different. We were standing at Piko Point in the middle of the night. There was no moon overhead, but I could see her in her Hawaiian print sarong as clearly as day. She was angry, hissing and spitting at me as she stormed over the lava.

"You don't get it! You bled! Right here! How could you be so stupid?"

"I bit my lip. It was no big deal. You should've seen Alika's nosebleed."

She whirled on me, flinging an arm toward shore. "Oh, I can. I can follow his blood trail from right here where you hit him all the way to the beach! Did it make you feel big to make the bully bleed?"

Yeah.

"No," I said.

"Bulai," she said, looking me right in the eye. "I know

you. You can camouflage yourself under an umbrella and hide behind sketchbooks all you like, but you're a predator just like he is. Admit it. You were thrilled when he ran."

Yeah.

"No," I said again.

"Lie to yourself all you want. It won't change who you are or the fact that you bled right here where the biggest predator of all comes to shore."

I snorted. "Whatever."

She looked at me with eyes wide and unbelieving. "One drop is all it takes. Kalei's onto you. If not now, soon!"

"Dream Girl—"

"What? What did you call me?"

I blinked, nonplussed. "Dream Girl," I said.

"Dream Girl?" she echoed. "Is that what you think I am?"

"Well, yeah."

She swelled, bringing herself to her full height. "My name is He-Kai-Le'ia. My family calls me Le'ia."

"Le'ia," I repeated. "My name is—"

"I know your name, Alexander Kanoakai Westin. And I know you. The problem is, you don't know yourself."

"I don't understand."

She laughed, short and sharp. "No, you don't. You don't have a clue what you've undone—all the years of careful planning and sacrifice—*my* sacrifice—it makes me want to cry. Talk is cheap. I'm done." She twisted the ti leaf lei off her wrist and threw it at me. "Here. You need this more than I, brother dear." She reached her arms over her head and flung herself into the big saltwater pool.

"Leʻia!" I stepped to the edge and looked down into the water. A piece of Hawaiian print fabric floated to the surface. Below it, heading out through the tunnel to the deep water on the Nalupuki side was the sleek bullet shape of a small Niuhi shark.

Epilogue

~Malihini: a newcomer to Hawaii.~

"Just my driver's license?"

"Yeah. The photocopier's over there."

Justin Halpert lifted the lid to place his card against the glass and a newspaper clipping slipped out. He bent over to pick it up.

"Oh, sorry," said Mrs. Thompson jumping up from her desk to help. "Nobody uses that photocopier much. They like the bigger one in the staff room. It's faster when you've got a lot to copy." She glanced at the paper in Justin's hand and clicked her tongue. "This belongs in a new student folder. It's probably been sitting there since April. Marie must have left it when she started creating the new student profiles for the faculty. You'll get yours next week."

"Marie?"

Mrs. Thompson grimaced. "One of the scholarship students. You'll find most of our students are here on scholarship. A few years ago the Board of Trustees got the bright idea of requiring a few hours of service a week in exchange for tuition. It's supposed to cut costs and give kids real world experience, but it's really more work for me. Marie was assigned to help in the office last year. Brilliant mathematician, but I swear she didn't know her ABCs. I'm still straightening out the files. But don't worry, she graduated last week, thank goodness."

Justin smoothed out the paper, turning it toward the light. "Jay Westin's a student here?"

"Incoming seventh grader. Big into surfing. That article was published back in February. Word on the circuit is he's one to watch. Might go pro."

"Really?"

She shrugged. "My son surfs."

"That board is amazing."

"Yeah. Everybody knows Jay's board. I think there are color photos of it in his application folder." She walked back to her desk, opened a drawer, and pulled out another file. "Here's his portfolio."

Justin walked over to Mrs. Thompson's desk and spread the folder across it. The shapes and colors dazzled: stylized surf scenes, a realistic portrait of an old man walking on the reef with a dog, a fantasy sequence with a girl in a swirling red cape, photos of wood carvings of a shark and turtle, and more photos of the surfboard, the green and browns of the shark-jaw lei snapping off the pages. "He's an artist?"

"Wondering if you'll get to teach him?"

"He's talented. Very talented. The way he uses color reminds me a little of myself at that age. Sixth grade when these were taken?"

"Check the back."

Justin flipped over a photo of the turtle carving. "Wait a minute. I thought you said his name was Jay?"

"Yeah. James Kapono Westin. Goes by Jay."

"Then who's Alexander Kaonakai Westin?"

"What?"

"These all say Alexander Kaonakai Westin on the back. This one also says Young Artist Showcase #93."

"Alexander Kaonakai Westin? I remember that name!" Mrs. Thompson walked to the large bank of filing cases and opened the one labeled Admission Applications. She ran her fingers along the top until she found the one she wanted and slowly worked it out of the over-stuffed drawer. "Here's his file." She laid it next to Jay's and opened it. She shuffled some papers, pulling one to the top. She slammed her finger down on the Final Waitlist Candidate sticker at the top. "That's why it rang a bell. He was waitlisted on the finals list!"

"Was?"

"We didn't accept him. Looks like we were waiting for art samples that never came."

"You mean the ones in Jay's file?"

Mrs. Thompson flipped through some more papers, comparing notes from each folder. "Same last name," she muttered. Her eyes widened. "Brothers! Jay was selected for early admission and Alexander's application was held pending review of his artwork. Confunit, Marie! That babooze filed the art samples in the wrong folder!"

Twenty minutes later Justin was aligning the contents of both files with the edges of the big conference room table, building his case. At the opposite end of the table, Mr. Ramos, Head of School and Justin's new boss, was working through the art photos. Having said her part and wringing her hands, Mrs. Thompson left, determined to double-check each and every file unfortunate enough to have been handled by Marie.

Mr. Ramos tapped the last photo. "You're right, Justin. He's got a gift."

"When you approached me in California, you said the Ridgemont Board of Trustees had charged you with creating a superior arts program."

"We want what you established in California—programs that consistently place graduates in the finest art programs in the world." Mr. Ramos reached for another photo, placing it in the middle of the table.

"You promised me if I came you would do whatever it took to make Ridgemont's art program world-class" Justin said.

"And I will. Whatever you need."

"The truth? You've got amazing studios and equipment here, but all the art supplies in the world cannot make mediocre talent great. World-class begins with talent. It begins with a gift."

"Justin, I know where you're going with this. Admissions for next year are closed. We're full."

"All I need is one shining star, one kid who breaks into the local art scene and inspires other gifted students to apply. If you want a world-class arts program, you need to attract young, world-class talent. To build this art program, I need Alexander Westin. *Ridgemont* needs him."

Mr. Ramos adjusted his glasses and frowned. "Every year we have to turn away talented kids. The differences between our final waitlist selections and those that don't make it are miniscule. But we still have to choose. We only have so many seats, Justin, and next year's are all filled. He'll have to apply for ninth grade. We'll green light his application for early acceptance."

"That's too late."

"It's two years."

"This isn't talent, this is a gift. Two years is forever."

"Justin, admissions for next year are closed. The letters went out weeks ago. I can't—"

"Can't what? Make an exception, admit a mistake, and let a deserving kid in? He met all the academic standards."

"Yes, but—"

"Look. Just look. A sixth grader with no training made these images. Made this art."

"Yes, but—"

"Are you telling me that if these images hadn't been placed in the wrong folder, you still wouldn't have accepted Alexander?"

"No," said Mr. Ramos with a sigh. "We knew he was in the Young Artist Showcase, but the admissions committee never reviewed the art samples. If we had, his application would have moved to the top of our waitlist and we would have accepted him. No question. But we didn't see them, Justin. We expect a high degree of commitment and follow-through in our applicants and their parents. His portfolio was incomplete. That's a big red flag. The deadline came and we had to make a decision. Someone else filled that spot." Mr. Ramos removed his glasses and rubbed his temples. "In order to reconsider Alexander, we'd have to remove someone else from the class. I'm not willing to do that."

"If Ridgemont's goal is to change the world through education, we to need start here, right now. Change this kid's world."

"What part of *the class is full* is difficult for you to understand?"

"How much room could one skinny kid take up?" Justin crossed his arms and glared.

Mr. Ramos just shook his head and sighed. "I wanted a world-class arts program, not a world-class pain in my 'okole."

"Sorry, I don't speak Hawaiian."

"You know what I mean. Are you always going to be such a pain?"

Justin shrugged. "When it comes to students and art, probably."

Mr. Ramos ran his hands through his hair, then polished his glasses on his shirttail. "All right," he said at last. "I'll have to run it past the board, but I don't see them objecting to—what did you call him?—'a shining star in the art world.' He qualifies for a financial aid scholarship, so I'll have to move some money around in the budget, and you better pray we can find another gym locker and seat on

his bus route. But he's it, Justin, no more! I don't care if you find Michelangelo under a palm tree in Waikiki; he'll have to wait; we're beyond full. I'll tell Mrs. Thompson to call the Westin family and send a follow up letter. But so we're clear, you have to be the one to tell Mrs. Nakamura that the seventh grade class schedule needs to be adjusted. I've faced enough dragons today."

WHISTLING ON HIS WAY BACK to the art studio, Justin carried a small package the size of a book like it was spun glass and fairy dust. At his desk, he grabbed a pair of scissors, cut a slit, and delicately removed an oil painting in a simple tabletop frame. He gazed at the portrait for a moment, pleased with the way the light fell on a beautiful Hawaiian woman reclining on the beach. The floral patterns and colors of her sarong echoed the sunset clouds above her, and her eyes were looking at something off in the distance.

A Mona Lisa smile, he thought. *I never knew what she was thinking.*

He set the portrait on his desk where he could turn and lose himself in moments of quiet contemplation, just as he'd been doing every day for each of the twelve years since he painted it.

"No matter how long it takes or where you hide, I'm going to find you, Pua," he said. "Promise."

GLOSSARY OF HAWAIIAN AND PIDGIN WORDS AND PHRASES

5-4-4 | A play on words meaning "go to the bathroom." When spoken, the numbers 5, 4, 4 in Japanese are go-shi-shi. Shi-shi is also how little kids say "pee."

'a'ole pilikia | No trouble; it's no problem.

ae | Yes.

'aina | Land.

'alas | Masculine family jewels.

'au'au | To bathe or swim.

'aumakua | Guardian spirit of an ancestor that can take many forms, such as animal, bird, fish, rock, or wind.

'okole | Butt; rear end.

'olapa | A type of tree.

'olohe lua | A Lua master, head of a Lua school.

'ono | Delicious; delightful.

'opihi | A type of limpet.

'ukulele | A small four-string instrument similar to a guitar. Literally translated it means "leaping flea."

'ukulele | A small, usually four-string instrument similar to a guitar or mandolin.

ahi | Tuna, a type of fish.

ai ka pressah | Refers to overwhelming sense of stress or performance anxiety; literally translated it means "Oh, the pressure!"

akamai | Smart.

akua | God; na akua means gods.

Ala Moana | A giant outdoor shopping mall near Waikiki.

an'den | And then; meaning "So what?" or "What's next?"

anykine | Any which way or style; also confused or uncaring.

auwi | Ouch!

babooze | A fool; someone who is stupid or goofy.

bamboocha | Big, huge, ginormous.

bento | A box lunch that can contain lots of different things like fish, chicken, beef, or pork as the main dish and usually includes rice, pickled vegetables, seaweed, and other local delicacies as sides.

boroz | The oldest, most worn-out clothes; one small step above rags.

brah/braddah | Slang for brother.

bulai | A lie; literally a "bull lie."

bumbai | Sometime soon; in the near future.

char siu/Char Siu | Chinese-flavored barbequed pork often used as filling for manapua or as a garnish for saimin. Also a nickname for Charlene Suzette Apo.

chasemaster | A game similar to tag.

chee | You think so? You notice?

cheehooooo | Wooohooo!

chicken skin | Goosebumps; an eerie feeling.

chillax | Combination of chill-out and relax.

choke | Lots; plenty; more than enough.

cockaroach | To steal or take something, to act like a cockroach. Literally "cockroach."

codeesh | Good grief; sheesh.

confunit | Exclamation of frustration; literally translated it means "Confound it."

cuz | Cousin.

-dem/-dem's | Refers to a group of people or things identified by one part of the group. For example, if Greg, Linda, Tina, and Josh were at the beach, you could say Greg-dem are at the beach. Literally "them."

fo'days | A very long time; too long. Literally "for days."

fo'real | Said to question or establish truth, reality, or teasing. Literally "for real."

grind | Slang for "eating," "to eat," "to eat very quickly."

guaranz | Slang for "guarantee," "no doubt."

halau | A dance troupe and/or school, usually of hula.

hammajang | Mixed up, broken, confused, junk, every which way. Usually describing something old and used.

hanabata days | Youth; small kid time. Literally the time when your nose ran.

hanai | Adopt; adopted; to adopt into a family.

haole | A white-skinned person.

hapa | Half.

haps | Slang for "What's going on," "What's up." Literally means "happenings."

haumana | Student.

haupia | A thick coconut pudding usually served in slices.

Hawaii nei | All of Hawaii, encompassing all the land, people, and traditions.

head mauka | To go toward the mountains. Mauka is the opposite of makai, which means to go toward the sea.

ho'i hou | To return; in Lua, it refers to the concept of looking to the past to understand the present.

ho'omau | Always; steady; perseverance.

honi | Kiss.

howzit | Hello; hi. Literally means "How's it going?"

huhu | Annoyed; angry.

hui | A group or club. Also to call out to get attention or to gather people together.

hukilau | To fish cooperatively as a group with a large net. Literally "pull ropes."

hula | A style of dance native to Hawaii.

hula halau | A school or group formed to study and perform hula.

Ilima | The name of a delicate orange flower and also the name of Uncle Kahana's poi dog.

imu | An underground oven, a pit where heated rocks and food are layered and covered until the food is cooked; similar to a clambake.

Iolani | The name of Zader's kite. Literally translated it means "heavenly (royal) hawk."

j'like | "Just like."

Jawaiian | Refers to Hawaiian music performed to a reggae beat. Literally "Jamaican Hawaiian."

kahuna | One who is an expert in a skill, labor, or body of knowledge. Also a priest, sorcerer, wizard, or minister.

Kailua-Kona | An area on the Big Island.

kala | Cash; currency; money.

kalua pig/pork | Kalua refers to food cooked in an underground oven or in that style.

kama'aina | Native born; local. Literally "land child."

kanaka/ kanakas | A person; a human being. Usually refers to someone Hawaiian or part Hawaiian.

kane | Male; man.

kaona | The hidden meaning of a song, poem, chant, dance, etc.

kapa | A type of cloth made from mulberry bark. Also refers to modern fabric with ancient Hawaiian designs.

kapu | Forbidden; secret; sacred; holy; not allowed.

kaukau | Slang for "food" or "to eat."

keiki/keikis | Child/children.

Keikikai | Family/kids' beach.

kikepa | A long, wide strip of cloth, like a sarong worn by women under one arm and over the shoulder of the opposite arm.

kine | Kind; type; style.

koa | A type of hard wood indigenous to Hawaii used to make surfboards, weapons, furniture, bowls, etc. Also a warrior.

kokua | Help; assistance.

kolohe | Mischievous; naughty; a rascal.

kukae | Excrement.

kulikuli | Noisy; deafening; meaning "be quiet," "keep still," or "shut up."

kulolo | A thick taro and coconut pudding often served in slices like fudge.

kumu | Teacher.

lanai | Porch; patio.

lau lau | A wrapped package of ti or banana leaves usually containing pork, chicken, fish, and/or vegetables and baked in an imu or in that style.

lauhala | Pandanus leaf. Used to weave hats, mats, bags, etc.

lehua | A type of flower sacred to Pele. It often looks like a red puffy ball. Picking it is said to make it rain.

li'dat | "Like that."

limu | A general name for all kind of plants that grow in water, usually referring to edible seaweed.

loco moco | An island dish with sticky white rice, a hamburger patty, and a fried egg covered in brown gravy.

lolo | Feeble-minded; crazy.

lomi lomi salmon | A dish made with salmon, onions, and tomatoes. Lomi lomi means "to massage."

luau | A Hawaiian feast.

lua 'ai | A hold, move, or form in Lua,

Lua, lua | A type of dangerous hand-to-hand fighting in ancient Hawaii whose holds and techniques are considered sacred and secret. Modern usage of the word also refers to a bathroom.

mahalo | Thanks.

mahalo nui loa | Thank you very much.

maika'i | Good.

maile lau li'i | A type of vine that grows in the rainforest. Very fragrant.

make "A" | To screw up; embarrass oneself.

make die dead | Poetic way of saying "very, very dead."

malihini | A newcomer to Hawaii, sometimes referring to tourists.

mamo | Hawaiian sergeant fish.

manini | Small; tiny.

mano | Shark.

Mele Kalikimaka | "Merry Christmas" in Hawaiian.

momona | Big; fat; large. Usually not complimentary.

nalu | Ocean wave; in Lua, it refers to acceptance of things you cannot change or control, like an ocean wave.

naupaka kahakai | A shrub that grow along the beach.

niele | Nosey; to keep asking questions; busybody; curious in a rude way.

Niuhi | Man-eating shark.

nyah | The sound made when sticking out your tongue.

ohana | Family.

ohana nui | Extended family; clan.

oli | Hawaiian chant that is not danced to.

opu | Stomach; tummy.

pa lua | School for Lua training.

pao'o | Hawaiian name for blennies, a small fish commonly found in tide pools.

pau | Finished; done; completed.

Pele | Fire Goddess.

piko | Bellybutton; navel.

Piko Point | The farthest tip of land on the lava flow between Keikikai and Nalupuki beaches.

pilau | Rotten; rank; stinky; rancid.

pilikia | Trouble.

plenny | "Plenty."

Pohaku, pohaku | The name of a guardian stone; the Hawaiian word for "stone."

poi | A paste made from cooked taro roots mashed with water.

potato-mac salad | A combination of potato and macaroni salad; a staple in Hawaiian-style plate lunches and picnics.

Pu'uwai | A town on the island of Ni'ihau.

puka | A hole; dent; ding. Also a door or opening.

pupule | Crazy.

shaka | A hand gesture meaning "hello" with thumb and little finger pointed out and other fingers folded into the palm.

shambattle | A type of dodge ball game.

shibai | A lie; a fib; a story.

side-eye | In a conversation, a look that begins with narrowing eyes that are sometimes shifted slightly off center and is used to convey meanings ranging from "are you kidding?," "are you lying?," "behave," "I know you're hiding something," "there's something we're not saying, but both understand," "something's not right," and "do you get the secret/joke/message I'm sending?" As with many Pidgin words, context and body language changes meaning.

slippahs | Flip-flops; thongs; rubber beach sandals.

stink eye | A hard, scornful glare or lingering dirty look.

tita | A tough girl.

titah | A term of sisterly endearment.

tutu kane | A term of respect used to address an older man; grandfather.

tutu wahine | A term of respect used to address an older woman; grandmother.

uhu | A kind of parrot fish.

uwehe | A hula move: while hips sway, one foot is lifted and the dancer's weight shifts as the foot is lowered, followed by both heels raising and pushing the knees out, followed by the alternate foot being lifted, etc.

wahine | Female; woman

Waikiki | A tourist area on Oahu.

wana | A spiky sea urchin that lives in crevices in the shallow reef.

wassa mattah | "What's the matter?" Often followed by "like beef?"

Discussion Guide

Spoiler Warning: These questions may reveal important details about the story. Be sure to finish the book before reading on.

1. In *One Boy, No Water*, family ties are important. How do the characters show they really care for each other?

2. Zader's allergies set him apart from the other characters. What are some of the things Zader does to cope with feeling left out at times?

3. Uncle Kahana teaches Jay, Char Siu, and Zader that there is no shame in running away from a physical conflict. Do you think it's better to fight or flee if you can? What if you can't run away?

4. Zader, Char Siu, and Jay all want to get a scholarship to Ridgemont Academy, but Zader doesn't get accepted to the school. Have you ever wanted something badly, but didn't get it? How did you deal with your feelings and the situation?

5. In the story there are questions and hints about Niuhi sharks, a man with too many teeth, a shark that's missing part of his tail fin, Dream Girl, Pua, and Zader's biological parents. How do you think these things are connected?

6. Why do you think Zader is allergic to water, rare meat, and seafood? Why does he have strange dreams?

7. Trouble comes for the characters in *One Boy, No Water* like ocean waves. What are some of the challenges the characters face? How does the book suggest trouble should be handled?

8. Have you ever seen someone teased for being different? How do you think that person felt?

9. Uncle Kahana asks Zader which is more important: what people think about him or what he can do. If Uncle Kahana asked you this question, how would you answer? Would you stay safe in the house or would you wear funny clothes so you could be outside?

10. If you could change one thing about the story, what would it be? Why?

For more classroom materials and information about Hawaiian culture, history, and island living, please visit www.NiuhiSharkSaga.com.

Acknowledgements

No book ever makes into a reader's hands without the support and hard work of many people, and *One Boy, No Water*, Book One in *The Niuhi Shark Saga*, is no exception. I am grateful to the following:

Kevin, my husband of twenty-five years, and our two kids, Dylan and Shelby, for their patience while Mom writes "just a few minutes more" for hours on end. Without their belief in me and willingness to sacrifice clean laundry and hot meals, this project would never have gotten off the ground.

My parents, Steve and Kathy Covalt, who funded my education and didn't roll their eyes too much when I announced I was going to be a writer, not a lawyer. My siblings Heidi, Jeffery, and Susan who promised to buy my book in the same breath as asking when the audio version was coming out. Also the entire Parker 'ohana who listened to me talk about this project ad nauseam at every family gathering for most of a year.

Corey Egbert, illustrator extraordinaire, who helped bring my characters to life.

The entire crew at Jolly Fish Press, especially Christopher Loke, executive editor, who first saw potential in my rambling book pitch, and D. Kirk Cunningham who introduced me to the art of twenty-first century publicity and the power of social media. Also The Heber Valley Writers Group who read pieces and parts and asked for more, and ReBook in Midway who provided a welcoming place to meet.

I owe a deep debt of gratitude to Princess Bernice Pauahi Bishop whose vision and legacy endowed and established The Kamehameha Schools where I first learned to write, as well as to Mary Kawena Pukui, Bishop Museum Press, and many others who preserved and continue to preserve Hawaiian history and culture for posterity. Any inaccurate portrayals are a result of my own imagination and imperfect memory—e kala mai ia'u.

Finally, words fail when I try to express how thankful I truly am for all the knowledge I have gained over the years from teachers, kupuna, and friends about Hawaiian history and culture and what it means to be a modern Hawaiian. To all these people too numerous to name, mahalo nui loa from the bottom of my heart.

ABOUT AUNTY LEHUA

Parker, aka "Aunty Lehua," is originally from Hawaii and a graduate of The Kamehameha Schools and Brigham Young University. As an advocate of Hawaiian culture and literature, her writings often feature her island heritage and the unique Hawaiian Pidgin. So far, Parker has been a live television director, a school teacher, a courseware manager, a sports coach, a theater critic, a SCUBA instructor, an author, a web designer, a mother, and a wife. She currently lives in Utah with her husband, two children, five cats, two dogs, seven horses, and assorted chickens. During the snowy winters she dreams about the beach.